D0912611

WOMAN BETWEEN MIRRORS

THE TEXAS PAN AMERICAN SERIES

Woman Between Mirrors

HELENA PARENTE CUNHA

TRANSLATED BY
FRED P. ELLISON and NAOMI LINDSTROM

University of Texas Press, Austin

First Edition, 1989

Originally published as *Mulher no Espelho*
Copyright © 1983, 1985 by Helena Parente Cunha

Requests for permission to reproduce material from this work
should be sent to Permissions, University of Texas Press, Box 7819,
Austin, Texas 78713-7819.

The Texas Pan American Series is published with the assistance of a
revolving publication fund established by the Pan American
Sulphur Company.

♾ The paper used in this publication meets the minimum
requirements of American National Standard for Information
Sciences—Permanence of Paper for Printed Library Materials,
ANSI Z39.48-1984.

Library of Congress Cataloging-in-Publication Data
Cunha, Helena Parente.
   [Mulher no espelho. English]
   Woman between mirrors / by Helena Parente Cunha ; translated
by Fred P. Ellison and Naomi Lindstrom.— 1st ed.
      p.   cm.—(The Texas Pan American series)
   Translation of: Mulher no espelho.
   ISBN 0-292-79045-7 (alk. paper).—ISBN 0-292-79052-x (pbk. : alk.
paper)
   I. Title. II. Series.
PQ9698.13.U45M813   1989
869.3—dc20   89-14613
                                                                  CIP

TRANSLATORS' PREFACE

Appearing in 1983, *Mulher no Espelho* [*Woman between Mirrors*] by Helena Parente Cunha quickly attracted notice as one of the most thoroughly literary novelistic responses to the current discussion of woman's role and status. It had already won a Cruz e Sousa award in part for its ability to communicate a woman's perception and understanding of what she experiences. Antônio Houaiss, as spokesman for the selection panel, recalls that jurors were immediately struck by this "solid psychological synthesis of woman/ women without precedent in Brazilian literature, not merely for its possibly confessional aspect, but also above all its profoundly revelatory qualities, in language intensely suited to its aims." At the same time, the panelists recognized the author's achievement in elaborating an esthetic text out of this intimate raw material, honoring her successful "quest for transformation" of experience into art.

No doubt the English version of the novel will also exercise its most immediate appeal as the rendering of a woman's experiences—not a generalized figure of woman, but a heroine grounded in a particular set of conditions. This nameless but well-specified woman is the product of an upper-middle-class family in Salvador, Bahia (a city whose name evokes an enduring patriarchal order and the residual forms of a slavery-based society). As recently as thirty years ago, members of many families were born or married into a limited repertory of roles: the all-powerful father, the indulgent mother, mediator between father and offspring, the daughter with her artificially prolonged innocence, and the young man of good family who could count on his irresponsibility being dismissed as the expected sowing of wild oats. This standard of family life, now undergoing some changes, is seen in two versions. In the heroine's family of origin, the arrangement causes damage to those involved, but maintains itself intact and gives the impression of functioning well; the heroine for many years believes herself to have been fortunate in her upbringing. Her family of procreation begins by replicating this ambiguous success, but as the sons reach adulthood, their conflicts with the father become so severe that the heroine's traditionally feminine mediation cannot restore the appearance of harmony, and both the marriage and the parent-child relations collapse. At the age of forty-five, the heroine finds herself alone and forced to draw on unexpected reservoirs of critical intelligence and insight to rework the terms of her existence.

This sequence of events is communicated to the reader through a Pirandellian narrative arrangement. Determined to see herself in her entirety, the heroine stands between facing mirrors; during considerable stretches of the novel, she speaks from this literally reflective situation, considering the multiplied images that serve as auxiliary versions of her. Together with the secondary visual selves she gains through this exercise, she acquires a verbal alter ego for her interlocutor, counterfigure, and rival in a competition of claimed authorship. This is "the woman who writes me," a novelist too eager to write the heroine as a figure of female oppression in a work that, apparently, is the worst one might fear from the phrase *feminist novel.* As well as trying to *write* the heroine, to inscribe her in a novel, this well-meaning intellectual *writes to* (and hears back from) the object of her concern, offering her, in a gratingly pop-Freudian jargon, glib analyses of her problems of the moment. ("The woman who writes me" should not be assumed to be identical with another female figure of authorship, a featureless generator of text to whom the heroine occasionally refers, without sarcasm, as *my* or *the authoress.*)

"The woman who writes me" attempts to give the heroine a definitive account of her situation, but discovers that this supposedly downtrodden and brainwashed creature resists her and sets forth assertions that contradict and compete with hers. The heroine has a distinct advantage: she speaks as *I* (as neither the scribe nor the authoress ever can). Through her conscientious efforts to be true to her experiences and perceptions, she wields a power denied the scribe, who is scarcely more than a conduit for widely circulated notions. Equally important, the heroine is an individual with her own distinctive body, memories, turns of mind, and habits of expression; she comes to know herself and draws on her particular strengths in finding a way through and out of her crisis. Her spiritedly personal approach to her problems suggests not only that an abstractly international feminism of essentially U.S. and Western European origin will not serve all women's needs, but also that there may be as many suitable forms of feminism as there are women.

Perhaps the most striking feature of this fictional war over the source of the text is that the heroine's claim to authorship comes to have a convincing validity within the novel; after all, she is learning to free herself from other people's scripts. So, while *Woman between Mirrors* might resemble those self-referred narratives that lay bare their own fictionality and renounce its illusory possibilities, Parente Cunha's novel works to draw readers into the novelistic invention. *Woman between Mirrors* is altogether a twentieth-century novel, but it is also solidly in the time-honored tradition of engaging fiction, with a protagonist whose overcoming of trials is a welcome relief and cause for hope.

Helena Parente Cunha was born in 1929 in Salvador, Bahia, in Northeast Brazil, which figures importantly in *Woman between Mirrors*. A resident of Rio de Janeiro since 1958, she holds a university teaching post in that city's Federal University, where she was formerly Dean and is now Professor in the College of Letters. Her areas of academic specialization are Romance-language literatures, Italian writing in particular, and literary theory. While it was her first novel, *Woman between Mirrors*, that brought her to the attention of a wide literary public, she had been publishing poetry and short stories over the past decade, winning a critical reputation and literary awards for her collections.

Brazilian critics, in their efforts to present this author's work to the literary public, have repeatedly pointed out a feature that may indeed help orient an English-language readership as well. Helena Parente Cunha's work forms part of a well-recognized current of innovative Brazilian fiction. While one might trace this tendency back as far as Machado de Assis—and, in fact, comparative references to this exemplar of irony and narrative playfulness are apt to surface in discussions of Parente Cunha's work—the immediate and most relevant founding figure is Clarice Lispector (1925– 1977). The author of the short stories of *Family Ties* [*Laços de Família*] and such novels as *The Apple in the Dark* [*A Maçã no Escuro*] began a line of experimentation characterized, above all, by frequent shifts of narrative voice and by an interest in ways in which readers gain access to the workings of characters' minds.

The novel continues another current in Brazilian intellectual life: the recognition and interpretation of the nation's cultural debt to Africa. The heroine is, significantly, from Salvador, also called Bahia, once heavily dependent on the Portuguese empire's slave trade, and still a stronghold of African-derived folkways. The heroine's upbringing is entrusted to a black nursemaid or nanna who fills her imagination with a mythically embellished vision of Africa, its royalty, its tribal memories, whose messenger is "the wind from off the sea." Especially important here is *candomblé*, the religious cult synthesized from principally Yoruba beliefs and practices that, brought to Bahia by Sudanese slaves in the sixteenth century, comingled with Catholic religious culture. The novel refers particularly to Xangô, god of storms and lightning, and two of his wives, Yansan, warrior queen and mistress of the wind, and Oxum, Xangô's favorite and goddess of streams and rivers. During *candomblé* rites, these and other deities become manifest in the persons of dancing celebrants. A Xangô figure from the heroine's childhood, "the black boy, son of the cook at the house next door," first embodies the mythic Africa she carries in her mind. Xangô's medium in the *candomblé* ceremonies is "the good-looking black man," who helps the heroine reorder her thoughts in the wake of her adult crisis. The acknowledgement that she is "not all that white," either in her physical traits or her habits of mind, is part of the heroine's distinctly Brazilian process of healing. Her recognition of Africa in herself is seconded by the novel's many allusions to Afro-Brazilian myth; the reader should be alert to these reminders in references to mirrors, wind, water, thunder, lightning, lavender, seashells (used in telling fortunes), mango trees, colored beads, basil, musical instruments, dance, and ritual drums in the night.

A few words are in order concerning our approach to the translation. A reader of both the original Portuguese and our version will recognize that the English tends more toward the colloquial register of speech and, at certain junctures, is less elliptical in construction than the Portuguese, among other adaptations. Our earliest drafts featured a more literal and direct equivalence between original and translation. Rereading these first versions, we were dissatisfied with those portions—the bulk of the text—in which the heroine speaks. She had acquired an elevated English diction that gave the effect of self-conscious striving for a misguided ideal of lofty expression. In contrast, the heroine in her original Portuguese-language incarnation is unmistakably concerned with developing a form of expression that will help her understand herself and the forces that have shaped her situation. While her utterances at times possess lyric beauty, they never appear to have been formulated with this goal in mind. We needed to restore this appearance of artlessness and pragmatic functionality to the English version.

First, we deleted and replaced those English utterances that, while literally faithful to the original, were untrue in spirit through their too-notable elevation. For example, *Estou muitas* could not remain as *I am many*. Not only was this English rendering too showily lyrical, but it echoed a line from Walt Whitman, strengthening the impression that the heroine wanted to sound poetic. The more earthbound

So many of me became her English-language reaction to her infinitely multiplied images in facing mirrors. In this same category is our frequent transfer of pronouns from nominative to objective case or to reflexive forms. *Eu sou eu. Ela é ela* could not always remain as *I am I. She is she,* but at times became *I'm myself. She's herself.*

The search for a more understated form of speech, one less apt to draw attention to its own mechanisms, also led us to expand and make more explicit a number of expressions left cryptically unlinked and discontinuous in the original Portuguese. A number of these cases involve isolated nouns or pairs of nouns. For example, while *compactude* effectively communicates the heroine's experience of extreme depression, *compactness* does not. We had to shift to a somewhat bulkier and more continuous phrase, *like a ton of lead,* with its familiar ring. Occasionally we have elaborated complete sentences in English to convey what in Portuguese was stated elliptically. Thus *Lodo e lama no desalento de ultrapassar* became *A slimy ooze tells me there's no hope of getting through.* Our purpose in carrying out these expansions was not to provide more explanation and interpretation than the original, but rather to avoid utterances without meaningful resonances in English, as would have been the case with the more literal *Mud and slime in the discouragement of passing through.* The heroine, in Portuguese, never appears to be Delphic or hermetic in her expression; her outstanding characteristic is an effort to state her feelings, experiences, and insights in a way that will make sense and strike a responsive chord. To be herself in English, she had to be equally eager and careful to make herself understood in her search for self-understanding.

The Translators

WOMAN BETWEEN MIRRORS

WOMAN BETWEEN MIRRORS

Now, when my faces come into alignment, one over another, and the dates come together, I'm going to begin my story. Here, where my body intersects with the space of my images. I have something to say because I'm going to say myself to myself, like anyone face to face with memory or a mirror. No, I'm not going to write my memoirs, or my biography or paint my portrait. I'm a made-up character. I exist only in my imagination and in the imagination of my reader. And of course I exist for the woman who is putting me on paper. At home or on the street, people don't know me. Does anyone really know anyone else, flesh crying out from beneath the mask of the face, this polished, proper shell? When I speak, people think they think they're speaking to me. What throws them off is going by the outside, always identical or similar, to some extent fixed, and we're going by the outside if we mean the length of a day, or even of a year. The outside, the skin side, changes with the changing of the cells. Growth. Corrosion. Decay. What you see. What changes underneath the skin, no one sees, from tears to laughter. Dizziness. Leaping and flying. Plunging deep down where things are imperceptible. I'm not smiling when I smile, I don't smile. I'm not crying when tears run down the furrows of my face. The truth is that, on the outside, I have no connection with myself. I am not even speaking, when I speak. Only in my imagination am I myself. Just like everyone else. But not everyone knows of this. What we know, we don't know. Reality is what you imagine. I exist in my fiction. Here and now. Now, when my faces come into alignment, one over another, and the dates come together. Here, where my body intersects with the space of my images.

Here and now. Why not there and before? Why not? What is the distance between the face in the mirror and the mirror in front of the face where the boundaries blur? The real is the unreal, now and there. Why not? The dates come together with my images and I say I. But when I say I, I'm not the woman who is writing this very page. When I say I, I'm merely imagining myself. She is the one who is writing. And my face in the mirror? Who is it?

Who is the woman who writes me? I know, because I made her up. Meanwhile, she doesn't know me. She thinks that she has me in her hands to write as she wishes. Someone she knows all about. She will write me just as much as I let her. Me, I'm a character built right into her life. The woman who writes me feels lost, she can't figure out where I go, I'm an irresistible presence that keeps getting away from her, slipping away, nimble, confusing and dominating. Unintentionally, she begins to mix her emotions in with mine. Projection is inevitable, but it won't be from her angle of illusion. Or better, her angle of illusion will open up together with my mirrors. From now on, let's keep things separate. She is she. I am I. She has her problems. I have mine. If I exist in her imagination, she wasn't the one who created me. I have made myself. Afterward I invented her. Creatures flowing out of my imagination. She wants to get a hold on me. She can't. I escape from her words. Her anxiety. This is my way of getting away. I won't make fun of her impatience. I need her. For years I've been waiting for her to be ready to face me. Me, I'm a character built into her life. No two ways about it. No matter how often I'm put off. I persevere, I wait. She never cared, just went right on ignoring me all this time. But I've been waiting so long for the right moment that I won't let her slip out of the grasp of my will.

From memory and from the mirrors a face emerges. Little Miss Sourpuss, a wide bow in her short tresses, a broken china doll clutched to her tiny bosom. There I am, a nice well-behaved little girl, praised by my parents' friends. Their compliments bothered me, I knew I was not as obedient as they said, I was naughty, I got into fights with my brother. Suddenly I saw myself as a big girl, who can take a bath by herself, who no longer needs to be told bedtime stories before she goes to sleep. My father announces to his friends the birth of a male child. My mother all smiles, between sheets of embroidered linen. My nanna filling the house with lavender incense and shooing flies off the mosquito netting. I'm looking on and saying how happy I am. My little brother, all wrapped up in his baby clothes, with blue bows, boy colors, all pretty and soft, I must be very careful not to drop him, suddenly I'm a big girl wondering if the diaper pin has come open? I didn't want him to get stuck. The woman who is writing me has something she wants to say, she thinks some explanation is called for. She went through analysis, to alleviate guilt feelings, her phantom dangers. She came out of her treatment with a lot of pat answers, and she thinks that she can interpret my childhood reactions with some half-baked Freudianism that she has never in fact studied. She wants to say that my wish was precisely to prick my brother in that little piece of his anatomy that's different from mine. It's not true. She's twisting things around. I was quite happy, by my mother's side, my little brother on her lap, laughing and clapping his hands.

You couldn't be happy. He took away the lap that till then was all yours.

The woman who is writing me thinks she's the guardian of the truth. She gets her reactions mixed up with mine. I used to play with my brother and when I got angry, I was immediately sorry. But once he broke my china doll. The china doll with the pink face, the curly blond hair, the one that opens and closes her blue eyes, says mama and stands up. I complained to my father, your brother is little, he doesn't know what he's doing. In my hands the pieces of pink china, a piece of the mouth, the empty eye sockets, the works that open and close the eyes, the blue eyeballs beneath long straight lashes, stop crying girl, I want my doll, get out of here right now, I went right on crying, the faceless doll saying mama, hush girl, then I broke my brother's little ele-

3

phant. On purpose, right in front of him. As my punishment I was locked in the attic. My nanna came to see me, angel child, don't be stubborn, come on now, her black hand, nice and warm in its roughness, soothing my face, me asking her not to leave, I didn't want to be by myself, blow your nose, looking at me with tears in her eyes, don't be stubborn any more with your daddy. I was sorry I did it, I shouldn't have broken my little brother's little elephant. It was wrong, I could see it was wrong.

It was not wrong. You have to admit that your behavior was normal for a child of eight, deprived of her favorite toy.

No apologizing or rationalizing away what I did wrong, even as a child. It was wrong. I accepted it. The attic was dark, I was very scared. Especially when I heard the rats. I shrank back so they wouldn't gnaw at my feet. A bit farther off, the sound of the ocean, casting shells up on the beach. I liked to get my feet wet in the ocean. And pick seashells out of the seaweed at the edge of the beach. The noise of the rats. The rats. They've started in gnawing at my feet.

The rats existed only in your imagination.

The rats started in gnawing at my feet. Where did they come from? Where were they coming from? On one of the attic walls was a mirror rusted through in spots. I was suddenly afraid of my face in the mirror. I wanted to scream. Terrified, my hoarse voice couldn't make it through the mirror. The rats were gnawing at my feet. Let me out of here, daddy. I'll never break brother's toys again. I was ashamed whenever my father told guests how I had broken my brother's elephant. From then on, no one ever again thought I was obedient or well behaved.

You believe that the others blamed you, because you blamed yourself.

She's writing me but she doesn't know any more about me than I do. The woman who writes me, when she was a child and her father punished her, ran away from home and went to the beach to play. The wind from off the sea is blue. Canoes landing, sails unfurled, the fishermen hauling in the net heavy with fish, their silvery scales throbbing in the dark mesh. The blue wind rocking the waves back and forth, the moving mirror of sand reflecting the light. My feet went straight for the seafoam, I wanted a red fish, my nanna held my hand. As the waves broke, the shells would come and go, boiling in the foam. I would take the little shells home. The blue wind sliced through my hair, lifted up my dress. The wind from off the sea, comes from the sea, comes from afar. The *jangada*-rafts would disappear into the horizon. I was taking the little shells home. The shells that belonged to the Mother of Waters? Who is lurking in among the rocks, the rocks pounded by the sea?

2

The woman who writes me never heard the noise and felt the fear of rats. Rats are not part of her childhood fears. It's true that she too lived in the huge old two-story town house in Rio Vermelho, with ground floor and attic, but the rats haven't left their mark on her remembrances. She doesn't like to talk about rats. She's forgotten or pretends she has, that her father set rat traps with bits of cheese here and there around the house. As if there might not be rats nesting in the attic or on the ground floor of the big old town house in Rio Vermelho. She won't face up to the dry sound of rats gnawing, the awful sound of gnawing. It's so hard for her to get involved with my problem and she keeps wandering off in the blowing wind that brings her noises she can't identify, odors of other decaying things, nothing registers.

The rats often come and gnaw at my feet. I'm weighted down by my own body. When I try to walk I get nowhere. I try to run away, I fall down. I try to use a mirror to make myself see the rats are just made up. But there aren't any mirrors. And my feet? They're not there. The rats drown themselves in the ocean waves. From here I can see the ocean and a blue with no rats in it. Someone calls me. I don't answer, the voice caught in my own voice. Who is calling me? It's time to go to school. The convent school, where the woman who writes me also studied. She used to like to go and come by herself. Someone always went with me. Nanna, who was my brother's nanna and had been my father's nanna, would take me, come after me, from here on up to just beyond the Mariquita Square is dangerous. There's the streetcar line. It might rain. Nanna didn't want me getting my feet wet in the puddles of rainwater, she threatened to tell on me, to speak to my daddy, speak to my mommy. But she didn't and I would look at the rain, hoping for a storm. The storm didn't come and when it did, I loved to see the lightning flashes in the dark gray sky. Exploding in thunder. Nanna would be scared to death, running around to cover up the mirrors in the house. Mirrors draw lightning, don't you know that? Don't open this window, child. Mirrors draw lightning, I know. The black boy, son of the cook at the house next door, would go out in the yard and yell and raise his arms and say he was king of the thunder. He'd say he would make a lightning bolt split the mango tree down the middle. Nanna would cross herself. All mirrors in the house are covered up. The woman who writes me used to disobey her parents and play with the black boys and girls, children of the cooks and fishermen.

If some of my experiences went the same way for the woman who writes me and seem also to have gone just the opposite way, it's because we love to cancel each other out. Reverse images face-to-face in the mirror. The other side. Reverse is the same as the opposite side. Reverse is different from the same side. I'm myself. She's herself. Outgoing and happy, that's her. Sober and serious, that's me. She opens up, I close up. As a little girl, mainly, before my brother was born, I wasn't afraid of people, I would talk, I started shutting myself out bit by bit. Buckle up tight. Seashell winding into itself.

Just because she thinks I'm her creation, the woman who writes me wants to shape me, get me in her avid hands. I wriggle free and, if for a moment I seem to submit, right away I get loose and leave her there fooling herself. I'm the shape of my own push and pull, not hers. That's why it's so hard for her getting me down on paper. She can't follow me without trying to irritate me with explanations. She thinks I give in because of guilt feelings. She's wrong there. I just like to live in peace, I try to understand those around me. If I don't, I accept it. She's all full of rebelliousness that feeds her own guilt, disguised as arrogance and cynicism. She still hasn't resolved the problems of her childhood. I have. She and I, yes and no and maybe all mixed together. I accepted my father's liking my brother better. I accepted my husband's not letting me go out alone. I accepted living at the beck and call of my three children. I accepted, I accepted, the risk and the loss, and alone with myself came out the better for it. She used to run away from her parents' home, never got married, went out with a lot of men. The triumph and the danger, but alone by herself, she came out the loser. Which is more authentic? To cry out no, and make a big thing of it? To whisper yes, very softly?

Her feelings are all mixed up. Where she trips up is the point where her complications began. With her father. Her authoritarian father whom I adored and she despised. In truth, each has her own father. According to her, the difference is all in our reactions. Rebellion and submission. She doesn't know that the difference is in the identity of the two fathers. Absolutely the same, only different. One shouting is not the other shouting. Each heard the shouting at different times, though it was the same shouting, the same fight. I loved, and she hated, our father. Our fathers.

I don't want to tell about the woman who is writing me. I want to tell about me and me only. She interferes, can't keep things straight, gets me mixed up. I have my father whom I no longer have, because he died, but I'll always have him. I used to say that I was afraid of rats and she wasn't. I meant, in order to get along with my father whom I loved, I learned to live in order to love him. A very large father for my small eyes. I never completely saw my father. I didn't raise my head to talk with him. If he hadn't stooped down to my fear, I would never have seen the deep wrinkle running down the middle of his forehead. No, my brother was not an authoritarian. It was just that we had things all marked out for all time, he was small, I was big. If I insisted, I would be the boss. If I insisted and my father approved, that is. But a man is a man and a woman must know her place. I had an old nanna who remembered ancient stories that her mother used to tell and that were told by other mothers who told about distant lands, where there were buffaloes and buffalo hunters and tall drums and powerful gods and warm winds, where the king was black. The king was black like nanna, who was my brother's nanna and had been my father's nanna. I have a husband who the woman who writes me says is killing me day by day. I have three teenage sons she says have already killed me, even if I don't know it.

She believes that claiming to be free can change the natural order of things. All this fist-waving and sneering of hers is ridiculous and immoral. She can't defend herself because she cannot say I. But that's how I play the game. I am reasonable when I want to be. I want to keep getting a better focus on things. The more she writes me, the more I'll be myself. The fiercer, the harder. I need her.

My husband thinks I should live exclusively, totally, give my all for him. This makes me very happy. In my children's opinion, every mother is duty bound to devote herself absolutely to those she has brought into the world. This is the guiding principle of my life.

You can't keep on clinging to this absurd idea. One must be conscious of one's own rights, especially nowadays, in the late 70s, in a city like Salvador. A woman must react, not let herself be led by the whims and excessive demands of the family. You can't go on living like that.

That's the only way I can live. My own choice, my own way. The woman who writes me only half sees me, without clear outlines. Because she belongs to my imagination, I can see her outlines, her edges. She will live only if I imagine her. I will live only if she writes me. We find ourselves attached by a thin taut thread. There's no way to separate us. Because I chose to, I held out my hands and my feet for the ties and knots that bind me. The knots and the ties set the limits of freedom. My own choice, my own way. It's me who's saying yes to it every time. The woman who writes me, wielding her no like a goad, imagines she has discovered the meaning of liberty. She's as much a prisoner as I am. Being free by needing to undermine standards is the same as being a slave. She's a slave to liberation. My submission liberates me. When my husband gets home from work, he always finds me freshly bathed, clothes clean, my hair done, a bit of make-up on my face. Dinner is ready, even if the cook had a mishap. When he gets home, he wants me near him. To bring his slippers, fix him a drink, chat with him about problems at the office.

When your husband comes home, invariably late and at all hours, he doesn't even care whether you're neat. All he cares about is whether you have everything all ready, if there are guests, especially one he wants to impress, by showing off a well-organized home, a docile pretty wife. He wants you around just to wait on him, open or shut the window, turn the air conditioner on or off, massage his smelly feet, give him the allergy medicine when his nose runs. To chat with him about office problems! After the drink hits him, he starts in cursing you, finding fault. You're running your feet off, a lot you have to smile about.

The woman who writes me has no idea of the subtleties or of the give-and-take of married life. She doesn't understand that if I don't insist on having a social life, it's because I respect the moral principles of my husband, who is shocked by the excesses and licentiousness today.

Your husband's moralistic scruples don't keep him from watching porno at the movie house, much less from being friends with gigolos, prostitutes, and the owners of certain low dives.

The calm happy life I live irritates the woman who writes me, accustomed as she is to making light of traditional family relations. But that's the rock I lean on, what keeps me steady. The safe way to go. Peace and quiet, a proper time for everything. Everything in its proper place. My father with his unshakable convictions. In the yard, passionflowers opening all the way up right on time. The sunflowers going right where they should go. The mango tree, down toward the middle of the wall, between the two yards. Ours and the one next door. The black boy, son of the cook at the house next door, hiding and running along the wall. Clambering up the mango tree. Tossing me a mango that I didn't pick up so as not to disturb the natural order of things. Nanna herself was a part of that universe of inviolable laws, here she'd been my brother's nanna and had been my father's, and was the daughter of the nanna to my grandfather, with his whip, boots, and spurs. She always told me that a white girl shouldn't mix with black boys. The black boy, son of the cook at the house next door, his little head shaved clean, a medal hanging from a string around his neck, would sneak in among the mango leaves. Sitting on the wall, dangling his bare legs, he would suck on the mango and smile at me. A huge rat eying me lurking down close to the muddy wall. I went running inside to nanna's lap. Angel child, don't let a rat scare you. Her hand, nice and warm in its roughness, soothing my face. The black boys and girls, children of the cooks and fishermen, weren't part of the world my father was in charge of. The wind from off the sea was wafting the strong smell from the tideland. The children are playing on the beach, running and getting tangled in the seaweed. I try to walk and I can't. A huge rat slipped down from the mud-stained wall and came to gnaw at my feet. My feet all covered with sand and salt. The seawater came and went, the tide always turned right on time.

3

The woman who writes me has always tried to ignore me, efface me, as if I weren't there. That's why she didn't want to write me. Meanwhile, she spends all her time thinking about me, goes whole nights without sleeping. Little by little, I'm getting hold of her way of being so cocksure of things. Little by little, she'll give up her idea I never had my own life, strength and blood, sweat and nerves. Although I was always there, since Rio Vermelho and childhood. Since our garden and my father. A face in the mirror, the image reversed. Lately, she couldn't keep denying I was there. Her own life and death. Kicking and screaming she's dragged into writing me. She has never stopped knowing me, both down deep and on the outside. For a long time, I've had marks on my body from her jeering laughter. Many, many times I looked for her. She was afraid to come near me. I've known her since those bright-dark days in Rio Vermelho. Girl and sea. Garden and father. I invented her, which doesn't include knowing her completely. Knowing means knowing as well as not knowing. Being sure you'll never really know, inside and out. When we see each other face to face, irreversible mirror, we're not seeing each other face to face. We see each other in between. Not the shock of confrontation but a slipping underneath. The more she avoids me the more I hold onto her. The more I hold onto her, the more I belong to myself. The moment she thinks she has a hold on me, she's lost. I find myself when she knows she's lost me. No, it's not a game. It's a battle. When she gives herself over to the weaving of the text, she begins to lose her self-control, gets tangled up in the net I cast at every step. Until she's played completely into my hands.

Just because it's her way to push back when she's pushed, she thinks I go along with things out of weakness and lack of will. Really it takes a more deliberate effort to be consciously passive than to strike back. Rebelliousness is a leap, letting it all out in an instant. It's breaking away without the stabilizing force of a wait. The free and open choice of passiveness points to the slow and steep way up. Building it up bit by bit.

When my father told me not to go to the beach or the movies and made me stay home with my brother, I didn't think twice—I obeyed. No doubt I could have resisted and gone out against his wishes. Openly or on the sly, lying and saying that I was going to study with a girl friend and going wherever I liked. I couldn't stand seeing my father irritated on account of me. I couldn't stand deceiving him, when here he'd believed in me, trusted my word. I preferred not getting to go out to upsetting my father. A lucid and reasonable course. Between the two scales of the balance, I well knew the weight that would bring me pain. She chose the side with a different set of pains, without hesitation. The other scale of the balance. When father said you are not to go out to the Lighthouse Sunday night, she'd be there Sunday night, in a tight-fitting skirt, smiling at the boys. Father didn't want her hanging out on the Rua Chile after school. Every afternoon she'd go hang out, she knew exactly where to find, alone or in groups, her latest conquests, whether one-after-another or simultaneous. She talked back to father's outbursts and never missed a party or get-together. When he threatened, you'll be the death of your father, she didn't give in. Certainly it was blackmail. Meanwhile, deep down, she feared her father would die, after one of those scenes. How many times, coming home late, she would tiptoe up to the door of his bedroom, to listen to the rhythm of his breathing. If he died because of her, she'd commit suicide. She had it all planned. Her guilt feelings have gotten worse than mine. One kind of freedom is not to feel remorse. And she feels it, her heart is getting tired. Although she denies it. One day, she ran away from father's house and never came back.

My father's house, a safe harbor, for me it spanned the world. In silences and whisperings, my mother was part of it. At times, when my father wasn't home, I'd hear her singing under her breath and sighing, her gaze lost in the distance. They weren't what you'd hear on the radio, they were songs that only she knew, that spoke of love or of dancing, in a ballroom full of flowers. My mother used to repeat certain phrases. Rules for living. In the first place, her husband, second, her husband, third, her husband. After that, the children. Yes, she was quite happy. Sweet-smelling, she waited for my father to come home from work. She used to wait for him. Perfumes, silences, whisperings. Her tiny smile. I used to watch. From a distance.

4

I have my own guilt, all those voices crying out inside me, twistings and writhings in my underground recesses. My nanna used to tell me stories about good little girls who turned into princesses. My nanna had a light walk, noiseless, but I could always tell she was coming, from the tinkling of her medals, hanging on a heavy silver chain around her neck. When my father would come home, the medals tinkled loudly, angel child, don't act up, be a good girl so daddy won't say anything nasty. I wanted a story, just one, but it was time for my brother's bath and my father had already come home. Just one story. Girl, go to your room. I went. I'd hear my father scolding my nanna, demanding to know why the boy still hadn't changed his clothes. But Master, sir. My brother was splashing water on the floor, the medals were tinkling nervously, I was whimpering, the rats were coming and gnawing at my feet, I called out for my mother. She didn't hear me. She hurried by, full of perfume, taking the newspaper to my father. I came in, nobody noticed. He was putting his arm around her waist. I went back to my room. Without the story of the good little girl who turned into a princess. I did not call my nanna. She was giving my brother his dinner. I was whimpering, listening to the dry noise of the rats. No, they weren't rats. My nanna always said that there weren't any. But they came. They were gnawing at my feet. Outside in the hallways, the tinkling of medals, coming and going. Nanna would lull my brother to sleep. I was no princess. Who would come to call me to dinner? In my underground depths, all those many voices crying out, twistings, writhings, guilt. My mother's voice asking my father if she could have them clear the table. My mother passing by, full of perfume. My father's voice calling my mother. I don't hear what they're saying, they speak softly in the bedroom. They talk. They talked on and on. They laugh. They'd smile and smile. I'm crying, keeping it down. I get impatient when I call my husband and my sons to dinner and they don't come. I get impatient when they leave their shoes scattered around the house. Mainly when the shoes are covered with mud. My nanna always told me not to come into the house with dirty shoes. My mother used to clean my father's shoes and never got impatient. If I get mad at my husband and sons, I feel a guilt that gnaws me clear to the bone. Then I try to make it up to them. I'd like to be just like my mother, who never lost her temper with her husband and children. Except when I went too far. But she was right to then.

And aren't you perhaps entitled to be impatient with your children, with your sons who day by day are killing their mother? And why should you keep cool when your husband's going after you? Nowadays, for someone to be as subservient as you've gotten to be, the only reason is you've fallen prey to pathological guilt feelings. You feel the need to punish yourself. You know quite well that you didn't like your mother. You were jealous of her.

As you can see, the reasoning powers of the woman who writes me are extremely limited. All her conclusions are based on certain ready-made notions she picked up during her years on the psychoanalyst's couch. As he filled her head with ideas about the Oedipus complex, she supposes she'll be able to figure everything out with this same old cookie-cutter pattern. In reality, the relationship with my mother can't be reduced to liking or not liking her. My father was overwhelming, he crushed everyone around him. Lord and master. My mother's voice couldn't get through.

You didn't hear her because you thought so little of her. You thought that she didn't participate in big or little decisions of the family. You didn't understand why your father treated her with courtesy, when she was such an insignificant person in your view.

We were all insignificant around him, all powerful, commanding or counter-manding, and there we were, down at his feet, submissive, subjugated, subdued, submerged, subtracted.

Are you aware how much rebellion you carry inside you?

She, the woman who writes me, lives by and for her own rebellion, when she herself couldn't tell you what it's all about. She sees only one side of things. But each thing has many sides, each person has many voices. Many silences. You need to see the other sides, hear the other voices, feel the many silences. That way we'll know the truth is not the truth. Because I know that the truth comes to pieces in our hands, all our whys and wherefores can't shore it up, I try to understand and accept the whole mind-boggling thing of it. I don't even need to understand. I accept and welcome it, for me it's better not to go asking questions. I accepted my father with my mouth set in a straight line. I don't go into the whys and wherefores, just accept my husband and my sons. That's the way I learned from my mother. My widowed mother, whom I love and admire. Her way of speaking softly and seldom. Her dense silence. Her silence that says more.

If you've fallen into behavior patterns similar to your mother's, that's out of a desire to identify with her, a way you discovered as a child to be with your father. You say that you love your mother and, still, you never visit her nor do you have her over, even though you live close by. You're repressed because you don't want to have your way, and you get more and more frustrated and dissatisfied.

You can see clearly that the woman who writes me is only able to see me from the narrow angle of her myopia. Although her need to get hold of me is stronger, she can't reach me for all her painful straining after me. She's suffering in my hands, deluded and distraught, and she thinks she's now in a better position to grasp me. She fails to see that love also has many sides and many voices. Many silences. Only those who experience love to the depths can understand that they're paid back a thousand times over for their sacrifice, the joy of suffering from so much love. It's because I love them a great deal that I divide myself among my husband and my three sons. Each in turn challenges the other over me. To love is also to draw blood and to cause pain. There are moments when I have the feeling they are sucking my very blood.

Keep in mind that they do not love you. They hate you. Whoever fails to control will himself be controlled.

Their way of loving me is to bleed me. Torn. Shredded. Destroyed.

You are revolted and rightly so. Admit it.

I understand, that's all. My husband absorbs me. The boys feel short-changed, they're not getting what they need the most from me. They have a right to the attention that I can give them whole-heartedly only if my husband is not around. When they were little, they spent more time at home, had more time with me. They'd play. They'd fight. They could be themselves. I tried to listen to each one of them, to talk to each one of the three. To be there for each one of the three, understanding, making concessions. I did my best to see that they weren't jealous of each other, like me, the way I'd felt with my brother. What I offered one, I offered the others, too. And if one got a present, I made it up to the others with something just as good. I kept them from being frustrated or hurt. At first they accepted their father's authority and I got them to be docile and obedient. Gradually everything changed. It wasn't working, not exactly a failure, but there was complaint after complaint. They're no longer themselves.

They were never docile or obedient. Deep down in their hearts your sons are full of rebellion. Against their father's domination. Against their mother's softness. All your care, all your devotion, all your sacrifice went for nothing. Now they're killing you. They've already killed you.

It's not true. She doesn't understand me and she never will, because she never had any children. She had an obsession with wanting to be free. I feel free in my voluntary servitude. My sons rebelled because they weren't all set to go along with paternal authority, as I had been. Young people today follow other patterns. They don't try to understand and just go along. My husband never spared the rod. He thought he was supposed to bring up his children in the same way he'd been brought up. Lay on the leather and shout them down. My biggest problem was how to tone down his violence, without at the same time showing disrespect to their father in front of the children. The children reacted in different ways. They refused to study. The more they were punished, the less they cared about their studies. Their revenge for the whipping and shouting.

And you, in despair, studying algebra and biology to teach your children, studying psychology and education to teach your children to yourself. You'd spend your time trying to hide from your husband anything that might start a scene at home, for example when one of the boys threw a rock on purpose through the neighbor's window. If your children fight less now, it's because they are together less often, since they're never home. When they were little, you were always trying to separate them and keep them busy, telling them children's stories, reading children's magazines, fixing candy and snacks. They are not jealous of each other. They hate each other. Your own love didn't help them. They hate you. Your attempt to keep things fair turned out to be useless. If you bought a blue jeep for one, he'd say he wanted the red jeep. Meanwhile, the other would demand his brother's blue jeep and wouldn't consider your changing the color of the first one. When you were going to take them to the movies, it always turned into a huge problem, because each had to see the film that the others didn't want to see. You tried to hide everything from their father. The fights with other children on the playground of the apartment building, the complaints from doormen and neighbors, the business of the little girl one of them took behind the cars in the garage. You didn't know what to do when they started going out at night on the sly, while their father imagined they were asleep in their rooms. You nearly lost your mind when you found out that the oldest hadn't been to school for over two months. You were shocked to within an inch of your life to discover cocaine in one of their rooms. You don't discipline your children, you feel guilty, on the rare occasions when you get impatient with them, and you always try to make it up to them in any way you can; there's nothing you wouldn't do for them. You've always sacrificed for them because you want to punish yourself for all the things you imagine you've done wrong all through life.

I've let the woman who writes me ramble on. It's important that you see how she gets all the facts distorted and out of proportion. She gets carried away exaggerating, because she has to make repression out to be the cause of all problems. She spoke because I let her. In the game of I-she, I do the deciding. But I need her and, really, it's good to get a look at all these things through her eyes, even though they come out false. At any rate, whether I like it or not, these things are her business, too. She's my creature and she can't slip away from me. Nor I away from her. However much we disagree, we need each other like lifeblood. My sons, suddenly, are also her sons. She doesn't know this. It's unbelievable, but she doesn't know my sons are her sons. I'm the one who bore them, out of my own love. She raised them in the hell and craziness of her own life. And there you have them. Rebellious, but fine boys. After the difficult phase of adolescence, they'll come out well adjusted. We'll each talk about them the way we feel they are. They are the same three kids. In the same way, different. Differently the same. I must bear with the woman who writes me. She's really trying to follow me. Intolerably nervous. Unbearably tense. Knowing she has a painful, but fascinating, task on her hands. She can't get me out of her mind. Especially when she isn't writing me. Tonight, if she manages to fall asleep, she'll probably dream about the rats from my childhood. And her feet will feel the gnawing. She'll try to walk and won't be able to get to her feet. And she'll be afraid. She won't admit anything fazes her, but now she'll feel my fear. My panic will be hers now. When she hears the muffled sound of steps on the floor above, she'll remember my rats, will shrink back, unwilling to face her guilt. I'll bring her back to reality. She won't get away from me. Following me and losing me, she'll come round to herself. I show her the way she'll take and be lost. She will not resist. She was so sure of herself, now she'll come down off her high horse. I'm not looking for it to happen. Fate. She can't escape any longer. My win is her loss. Only when she fails will she be all the way herself. Her failure will bring my fiction to reality. I'll be that much more myself. Although. But the mirror.

5

I don't remember if I said that my husband likes to see me all dressed up. Nice clothes, my hair all fixed, just a touch of make-up. I dressed myself, but my nanna would brush my hair out and tie on a wide bow. What color? To match the corduroy dress. But you're going to be wearing your piqué dress. I wanted the bow to match my corduroy dress. This afternoon I'm going for a walk with my nanna and my little brother and we're going to Ondina beach. My nanna's crinkly hair is parted in the middle with two little braids fastened at the back of her head. Her medals were tinkling under her white starched dress. My mother passed by and smiled from afar. She's submerged in her silences, in her songs. I held my hair up so nanna could tie the bow. I also wanted to use my brother's lavender. Nanna said I could. Just a dab, angel child. When we crossed the street, I held nanna's hand. Hold tight. Nanna's hand was nice and warm in its roughness. My dress had a yoke with a pattern in piqué. My husband always likes to see me all dressed up. Even more. He doesn't want to see me get old. On the one hand, it's a good thing, it shows he cares about me, loves me. People say that I don't look my age at forty-five. But wrinkles do show up and it's not easy to hide them. Fortunately, I don't have to worry about dieting, thin as I am, with a youngish slender figure. My husband insists on my looking young. Smooth skin, gracefulness, alertness, lively bearing. A way for him to show caring, love. The woman who writes me would like to interpret this fact as meaning what he cares about is showing off his worldly possessions to the company employees or to the bank directors he's out to impress. Now I don't wish to hear the voice of the woman who writes me. I'm the only one speaking. Meantime, all she does is write. If my husband just absolutely can't see me as an old woman, with a saggy face, lines, that means I should feel more appreciated. It's true that this, at times, gets to be the hardest thing for me. When he puts on his glasses, pulls my face up under a strong light and starts to examine my skin, around my eyes, around my mouth, near my chin, at the bottom of my neck, around my ear, you have to do something about it. Yes, I have to do something about it. Massages, creams, beauty masks, I'll keep from smiling as much as possible, I'll quit crying, I'll sleep face up. I will do something about it. My nanna's hand with its nice, warm roughness would soothe my face. The son of the cook at the house next door, sitting on the wall, used to tell me he wasn't afraid of storms or lightning. Me neither. I wasn't afraid of storms. When my nanna used to cover up the mirrors, I always hoped she'd forget and leave one uncovered and a lightning bolt would come in the house. Girl, you don't know what you're talking about. Santa Barbara, we call on you. Santa Clara, send away the stormclouds. Santo Domingo, let the sun shine. Rain, rain go away. Make the sun come out today. I held nanna's hand wrapped around mine. If I keep from crying, besides being an exercise in self-control, it'll help ward off wrinkles. I look at my face in the mirror. Whose face is it? The photograph of little Miss Sourpuss. A wide bow in her hair. What color? Whose face is it? If I keep calm inside, my face will finally take on that easy confidence that certain women take on in their mature years and that gives them an irresistible allure, better than looking young.

You cannot believe all this foolishness. You can't fantasize this tranquil ideal, as if you lived some completely bucolic existence. Your allure is the sick attraction of a ghastly human rite in which you're the daily sacrifice.

I don't think life is a ghastly sacrifice. It depends on who does the living. In one person's case, a wart on a finger can turn into a catastrophe. Other people can be totally mutilated and it doesn't mean the end of their world. I don't think it's a massacre for my husband to want to find dinner ready when he comes home from the office. If I don't have an outside job, running the house should be my responsibility. My family, my home, my infinity. Keeping things the way they should be, orderly, on time. One of my strong points is cooking. She, the woman who writes me, has to make a big thing of the times when my husband and my sons got up from the table, without eating their food, grumbling or muttering angry words, throwing their food off their plates or onto the floor or at me. Yes, it's true, they acted like that, they did act like that, but it was only once, they were all on edge because of some problems with their friends, and furthermore they didn't actually hit me, I just happened to be near, the food fell on me accidentally, they're just naturally high-strung, touchy. Thorns and sharp blades. I accepted a responsibility in life. My family, my home, my infinity. I shall not fail.

You have already failed. From the very start, you failed by omission. Your running around making excuses for everybody and for everything. And your routine of self-condemnation and self-punishment.

My husband likes to have me near him. When he arrives, he finds me already waiting for him, sweet-smelling, keeping my voice low, or in one of my silent moments, not singing either.

When your husband arrives, you keep hoping he will take the glass of ice water, instead of that damned rum with lime you're supposed to make strong enough, and enough of it, to last the approximately two hours before the dinner ceremonial, when he comes to the table high or dead drunk and then anything can happen, like the time when he forced the housemaid to sit at the table to eat and then simply went to bed with her. And you! Where did you hide to pretend you couldn't see this depravity! How many times did he come home drunk and smash up the glasses and the china! How many times did he beat you up! Enough of pretending and fantasizing happiness that isn't there.

God! My God! Sometimes life looks all uphill. The way it just tears you up. I always manage to fight off the discouragement and fatigue that sometimes take their toll on me, weakness of will, and I don't always bounce back. Choking on a cement block in my throat. I sit down in front of the window, trying to get some air. Seven floors, from here to the ground. If I jump. To get rid of all this weight. Stone. Cement block in my throat. If I jump. The other buildings so close. The stone wall. Cement blocks and granite all around and over my head, and I'm cast in stone, stuck fast, hard, hammers and picks in my ears, I close my eyes covered with lime and soot, ash scattered all around me, the rats, the rats, the rats streaking by, making their rounds, I feel nothing, I'm cast in stone, cement caked down my throat, I'm sure that I can't vomit up a rat, they're making their rounds, ready to gnaw at my feet, I shrink back, no, I am not stone, the rats walk over my flat belly, their stubby claws scratching at my skin, tickling to drive you crazy, I try to laugh, let out a big belly laugh, that would help, the rats darting underneath my unshaven arms, but how could I have left my armpits unshaven? the rats tangled up in the hairs, no, they don't bite, they scurry over my curled-up body which can neither laugh nor cry, curls up tighter and tighter, the rats darting back and forth, scrabbling over my freezing cold skin all in goose pimples, sweat oozing out in driblets of dirty slime and soot, ash working into this putrid muck slathered all over my body finally free of the rats that didn't get at my feet to gnaw at them and went back into the cesspit dug beneath my armchair, ah, I can't get my eyes open, can't move, can't breathe this air that circles around my shoulders, all I need now is the soothing ocean roar, under my window. Under my window you can't hear the ocean, I can just catch glimpses between the buildings. An ocean cut off, way out there.

When I was a child, I used to pick four-o'clocks that grew in the garden at home and I would make necklaces and wreaths, being very careful to stick the tiny stem of one into the heart of the next. Often before I went to sleep, I'd listen to the rhythmic beat of the drums that came on the waves of the wind. I'd call for my nanna. The beat and throbbing that came in the night, from far away. I'd hold onto my nanna's hand. Tight. The drums of Xangô. Nanna would repeat, gazing off into the distance. The drums of Xangô. Who is Xangô? Go to sleep, angel. You're not afraid of lightning or of thunder. The black boy, son of the cook at the house next door, used to say that he was king of the lightning. Now he's sitting on top of the wall, right underneath the mango tree. Soon it will be night. He looks at me and smiles. The grass is all full of chirping crickets. I run after the crickets, without remembering that at the foot of the wall there is a hole where one day a gigantic rat came out.

6

I woke up with my head splitting, hot and feverish. The woman who writes me has let herself fall into such a depression she's lost her outlook on me. She's too numb and weak even to work up contempt and hatred. Burnt out. She sits at her typewriter out of sheer compulsion, her hands heavy, dragged down by my presence. My presence makes her squirm, she wants to escape but it's too late. I've sunk in under her skin. She started out across the abyss and got to where she'd be crazy to go forward and she'd fall if she turned back. I'm the abyss. If she leans over and tries to look down, she gets dizzy, everything goes blurry when she looks into my unfocused image. When she tries to get away, it's too late for her to pull her foot back from my precipice. I have her fascinated in my grip, all because I exist but she doesn't know as what. I'm a sore, painful image she claims to have worked out of her system. She loathes me, because I show to her what she has tried to write out of her story. She scratched away at it but couldn't erase it; you can douse the fire, but the scar is still there. Those burned-in lines are the map she didn't follow, turning her back on its fire. She chose to be gouged and ravaged a different way. When you reject your own dangers you can swerve off, evade guilt, but you still end up going down into the maelstrom. No one escapes from the greatest depths. Depth and death. She didn't know this. I'm the depths. I am the danger without the adventure, which she tried all her life to avoid. The woman who writes me thinks she's free of prejudices, completely open, mistress of her fate. She has fought her way through a lot. Saying no and all hell breaking loose. Being driven to find herself. The deluded notion that if she denied herself she could affirm herself. When we go against ourselves and knuckle under to whatever they lay on us, we're taking on a madder, bloodier task than when we shake off the yoke. The free life she chose didn't shake her loose from her phantoms. She may be a free spirit but she ends up paying for it.

Let there be no doubt about it. She, the woman who writes me, can't speak of herself here. Only I have the right to speak of her. With the freedom that comes from my fiction. If she wants to express her anguish or revolt, she'll have to go through me. The moment she says I, she isn't any more. Here, I can only mean me, I'm the only me. For her to say I, she'll have to invent herself, the way I invented myself. I set my own rules. My space and my time are mine to command. I need an extension of myself, my space, when I go out. I can't go across every street or pass every corner, although my trip back through memory is more flexible. Through memory and in imagination. It's not that I have special privileges that she doesn't. It's just that I get to set my own boundaries.

I and she. She and I. If we have lived apart so long, it doesn't mean there was any breakup. Our edges come together at the mirror we are always walking through, never getting cut. Even if it's in the dark. Despite the darkness, I see more. She doesn't see through my eyes. But she speaks through my mouth.

The woman who writes me is prostrate. She can hardly write me, her fingers just lie there on the keyboard. I'm what drains her energy. But even then she doesn't pull away from me or get up from the typewriter. Obsession and torture. As long as she doesn't go clear down to the bottom of the mirror, she won't ever be free of the precipice. In her fall, she will see me through her eyes, but there I will have overcome myself and I'll turn my back on her, me, at the crossover, me-with-her. Me-she, a fusion? Too soon to say.

No, she doesn't want to talk. I wait, but nothing. Out of fatigue or apathy, she gives in with no resistance, no wounds.

I can enjoy being free. Something no one knows or suspects, supposing that the only thing allowed is to keep in line. When I'm at home alone, I give myself the right to indulge in forbidden things. I sing my favorite songs, and nobody makes fun. I feel my freedom in my tastes and in my voice. And I dance, full of rhythm and motion. When my boys began to buy records, I really wanted to hear them and dance with them. All I got was laughed at. Disco for an old lady? I felt ashamed if the boys told their friends that I was on my last legs and imitated me, shrieking with laughter. That was the last time I went anywhere near their friends. She doesn't know what's what, that old bag. I don't care, just let it go by. At the times when I am really home alone, I lock myself in my room, turn on the record-player and start dancing. Sound pulsing through. I leap to the other shore, free of the knots and the rules. Moving with the heavy beat, my whole body comes together in a rhythm that goes in deep. I like to put on my forbidden dresses, the ones my husband called indecent. I smile, I'm in on this with myself. I plunge the neckline down low. Loud colors, special make-up. On my eyes, plenty of eye-shadow, plenty of mascara. False eyelashes. A wild tousle of my hair down on my forehead. The neckline still more plunging. Who is that sultry provocative woman in the mirror? It's not me. She looks like her, the woman who writes me. I keep on dancing, in my red dress, clinging, plunging, slit up the side, I hardly recognize the image that jumps out at me from the mirror. Is it she? Is it me? Which one is for real? This one, breaker crashing, facing me in the mirror, wouldn't blink at jumping into bed with a man she'd met just hours before. Which is the real woman? Which is flesh, which is blood? The one who looks at me from the mirror, a smile from the other shore? Or the one on this side, the good housewife and perfect mother, modestly dressed, just a touch of make-up? Where's the mask? On the scrubbed clean face or on the one daubed with false colors? When I pile on the make-up, am I taking off my mask? Or am I putting on my mask, when I wash my face?

All alone in my room, inside my mirror, me and me, I like seeing myself. Me? Her? Charming and pretty in dresses guaranteed to raise eyebrows, in her forbidden movie-star shoes, heels up to here, a slender leather strap running around her ankle. Who is she? Who am I? Under the flesh, under the blood? Alone in my room, I'm not alone. So many of me. For a few moments, I jump out of the circle I'm sealed into. They've got me closed in. The mirrors open the cracks through which I escape. The mirrors in the wardrobe doors of my room. I'm headed out in all directions. Presto, so many of me, taking every stance. I come and go, keeping an eye on the mirrors. That's me, along so many untraveled paths that flash open for me, offered up by the reflections.

In the throbbing rhythm, I claim my quota of freedom, enjoy a sensuality I never knew, take pleasure in a physical beauty that brings me back up. When I turn off the record-player, I go into the shower and let the water run all over my satisfied body, after the orgasm that I gave myself. The water rids me of so many fears, sloughs off so much dead skin, divests me of so many masks. For a few minutes that I stretch out as much as I can, I live my nakedness which comes out even more in the flowing water; the more the water runs over me, the more naked I feel.

I often take delight in seeing myself nude, alone in my room, in the mysteries of my body which the endlessly juxtaposed mirrors hold out to me, promise me, waft my way. I catch glimpses through the gaps of what has been denied me. Of what I denied myself. My nakedness attracts me, excites me, frightens me. The height of pleasure looking into mirrors that propel me to places never imagined. Inside the mirrors. I feel an orgasm and I'm not feeling one. Orgasms without orgasm. Day in, day out, a suicide slowly settling into me. Only in the mirrors does my sexual desire, which is bound to silence and to absence, speak out. I am nothing but this feeling that I don't feel. The cold that comes through me to become a shiver. The generous warmth that makes me throb faster and faster. I bare my flesh, my blood. I throb. I float free and wide. I am reckless, trembling all over, with every part of my body. I plunge in among my multiplied images and see my solitude opening up. My body is together with my body. I feel how morbid it is, searching for whoever's in me. I drift off across myself, leave everyone else behind. I am the center of my images. And my sex, what could it hope to find in this solitary encounter? With nothing to hold me back, I let myself be swept off, clear into pain. A drive toward betrayal. My flesh and my blood burn, eager to be cut and torn by the brutality of a crushing, shattering force. The man I have, I never had and he never had me. When he crushes me in bed, it's under the weight of his thick sweaty body, that can never conquer me or hurt me. I'm a self-watcher, without mirrors, neutral and ill-defined, giving in more and more. More? More and more? He goes in me and pulls out of me, as if he were not going in or pulling out of me. The sweaty stench of his fatness. Now, standing before the solitude of my mirrors, I look for him but nowhere can I see the man who would make me fall in love. I see him only in not seeing him. In this seeing not-seeing my images peer blindly into one another. My solitary breasts, my buttocks left unstroked, my desolate sex. On fire.

Ah, the woman who writes me is a bitch. She refuses to speak, lets me feel her desperate solitude to the hilt. Her free, immoral life never got her anywhere. Yes, immoral. Her body given to so many men, her thirst for love frustrated, too, with every experience. From man to man, she ran after the impossible. Not that she didn't have what it takes to be loved. Not that she wasn't made to the fit of love. Just that the quest for love shouldn't be a way of rebelling, can't be a chance to get even. The many men who tramped through her body, who cut into her flesh, nailed deep within it the sign of guilt. Which she tries to hide from herself. In the middle of my mirrors, sensing the desperation of her solitude, of her guilt disguised as liberalism and independence, I burst in on her immodesty. I shed my sense of shame and fears. Naked in the middle of the mirrors. I can't find myself. Where am I, all in bits over so many images?

No, I am not I. It's she in her indecency. She. The woman who writes me. She watches me and smiles. I come nearer. I'm right up against her cold face. The mirror. The mirrors. At this instant I have no control over her. I hate her. I close my eyes to keep from seeing that smirk on her face. She knows that now she can do anything she likes with me clutched in her claws. At this instant I'm out of my own control. At the mercy of desires with no answers. It's a denial of having lived. Why not come right out and say that you can live? Why desires with no answers? I open my eyes wide. Unafraid to look. I see. My body, smooth and slender, on my face a lascivious and lubricious smile. Now indeed, I am sure. This face is mine. My face. My face? No, no. This face is hers, the face of a loose woman. I close my eyes. I clench my fists. I advance. Against whom?

My hands are dripping blood on the pieces of the mirrors strewn across the floor. Blood stains the broken mirrors. Pain in my hands, sliced into by countless blades. I've lost all the faces. Pieces of face underfoot. In my despair I come into my own self. I?

$$\boxed{7}$$

The woman who writes me hears the sound of the rain and thinks of me. She wants to write me and she will, with her hands bandaged. Bloodstains on the gauze. I'm bleeding again. My body aches from the exhaustion that comes after a fever. I was in bed, I was so weak. Her hands bandaged, she's typing away. I don't wish to know why my hands are bleeding. High fever. That's come and gone.

When I was small and got sick, my nanna would sit at the foot of my bed. Her hand would go back and forth over my forehead, the medals lightly tinkling. She would give me sassafras tea and bead necklaces for my doll. I didn't want porridge. It has little round lumps in it, the way you like it. She would bring me tapioca pudding. I would hold my nanna's hand. The son of the cook at the house next door also has the measles. I didn't play with him because he was black. I didn't play with the boys who were not black because my nanna said that daddy didn't want me to play with boys. Girls only play with girls. The mango tree branches in the garden are heavy with ripe fruit. You can't suck mangoes because they're not good for you. Girls play with girls, boys play with boys. My boys always played with girls. And what if they do do something wrong?

You see evil in things that are simple and natural. For you sex has always been taboo. You don't feel any pleasure with your husband, not because he's heavy and flabby, but more than anything else because you see the sex act as something lewd, debauched. You quit having anything to do with the little girl who asked if she could show you her breasts that were just starting to grow in. You felt insulted when someone asked you if you had got your period yet. You used to tell your girlfriends at school that you didn't like to talk about such filth. And you didn't. When they started to whisper and talk about what you called immorality, you'd walk away. The whole time you were a single woman, you avoided using such words as lover or pregnancy around your parents. You were dying of embarrassment when you had to tell your parents that you were pregnant. Even today you look at the floor if anyone as much as mentions a simple honeymoon, it doesn't even need to be yours, because you yourself know what kind of sacrifice it meant for you and how it went against your sick scruples. If you don't feel pleasure with your husband, the real reason is you're hard and dry and not that he sweats and goes limp.

The one who is saying these crude, vulgar things is the woman who writes me, she never will accept that I'm shy and modest. It's good that she says what she thinks. One of my ways of leading her on. Although she believes that when I speak, I speak because she, in writing me, wants it that way. She simply wants what I want her to want, since I invent her each time she takes a hand in matters. I create myself so far as I dominate her. So far as she thinks that she dominates me, I create her. Each of us independent in our chains, enslaved but free.

When she was thirteen, she was already thinking about having a sexual experience, shamelessly undoing the last button of her uniform blouse, on the way out of school. At thirteen, I was asking the cook at our house where the egg came out of the chicken. From her astonished face, I knew I'd said something stupid. She laughed, didn't answer, laughing hard, I still hear it and always will, that laugh, a sharpened echo against the eardrums of my memory. The uneasy feeling, the sense of ridicule that covered-uncovered me. The newborn puppies from the house next door, the children showing off the whelps, this one's male, this one's female, there I was, looking hard, thirteen years old, looking and looking, I didn't have the nerve to ask how they could tell the difference. Afraid they'd burst out laughing. The girls in my class at school used to laugh at me. The woman who writes me also laughed at me. Wall of thorns. I felt different from the rest, I didn't know how to make the climb up any easier. My father liked for me to play with girls younger than I was, neighbor girls, and I would play blindman's buff, jump rope, run races, while my girlfriends were out walking to the Lighthouse, on the Rua Chile, Sunday matinees, parties at clubs, parties at private homes playing records, flirting, love affairs. Me playing around my front door. My girlfriends going by laughing. At school they'd tell each other. Wall of thorns. I was a paper doll. I collected picture cards from Eucalyptol soap, while my girlfriends were pasting up albums of movie actors. While they were wanting to wear tight sweaters like Lana Turner and tried to get their hair to go in a pageboy bob like Veronica Lake, I was still wearing my sailor suit and had my hair tied up in two bows. My girlfriends copied down the words to bolero and foxtrot music, I was reading books by Monteiro Lobato. I never had anything to talk about, that silly nitwit, paper doll, thin stiff little paper doll, face like an empty box. The woman who writes me even today still laughs at the paper doll, face like an empty box. Once some friends of my parents came by our house, a married couple and two teenage daughters I didn't know. Having company like that threw me into a panic so I could barely keep up my end of the simplest conversation. Fifteen years old. Paper doll, in the room where the girls were waiting for me, I was nowhere to be seen, didn't have the nerve to come down from my room, till my father came up, come down right now, I will, making my entrance only I didn't even say hello, all I managed, paper doll, was to ask the first girl, all I could ask her was, do you want the black pieces or the white ones? Everyone laughed and laughed, there I was, the paper doll, the checkerboard shaking in my hands, everyone laughing, me running to my room, my father explaining, she's been running a fever since yesterday, everyone ashamed of themselves, what a scene, paper doll, face like an empty box.

You think you're not rebellious because you keep quiet, don't blow up, but you ruminate, chewing on the pieces you swallowed without digesting them and that are still stuck in your vomit and in your nausea.

I don't vomit and I don't feel nausea, I merely remember what happened, wall of thorns, harsh, but it kept me on an even keel, fears and shame. Between girlhood and womanhood, I didn't manage to cross the dividing line. On one side, I didn't fit. On the other, there wasn't room. At a crossroads, heavy shackles on my feet either way, no way to move on, to stop meant going even more ridiculously backward. My feet dead weight for all time. I didn't know how to dance. I told my girlfriends I didn't feel like it. Same as when I said I don't go to movies because I don't feel like it. I don't go to the beach because I don't feel like it. I don't feel like it, don't feel like it, as if not feeling like it were my reason for never showing up. As if not feeling like it were more legitimate than my father's saying he won't let me. And he wouldn't. Why didn't I want my girlfriends to know that he wouldn't let me? And didn't I feel like it? Feeling or not feeling like it, what difference did it make?

Your father used to take you to the beach, there you were, fourteen, a paper doll. Come along to the beach. You'd go with him. Take your brother's hand. And you'd take it. Play with him. And you would. Don't let him go where it's deep. Finally, you let him go once. He almost drowned. Once more you showed you were ready to kill your brother. The first time was in the cistern in your backyard. Your fratricidal fantasies.

The woman who writes me brings up everything that comes into her head, without reckoning the consequences. I loosen the reins of her imagination, but she doesn't know how to deal with it or work free. Although she firmly believes that she's cut the bindings and the knots. I have her all tied up.

You're the slime at the bottom of the well.

She's the dirty side of my stain.

There I am, in a corner, with myself and without myself. Clinging to a clock, one of its hands moving ahead, the other backward. A corner with its own angle closing in on it. My heavy feet, with no ahead or before, with no further or beyond. I didn't know how to dance. Heavy feet. Cement feet. Stiff paper doll, who'd ever want to dance with me? Especially, where would I dance? The corners were closing into a single point. My father thought dancing was indecent. What a man feels when he puts his hand around a woman's waist. What happens in the heads and in the blood of a boy and a girl dancing in each other's arms. And really, why should I learn to dance? One day an invitation from a friend of my father's to his daughter's thirteenth birthday. Me, sixteen. A lot of girls came with their parents or without them.

A simple party with dancing, a record-player with lots of records, the same number of girls as boys, and I certainly didn't feel like going, knowing how it was going to be set up, I didn't want to go, what would I say if I got asked to dance? as if someone were to ask me to dance, stiff paper doll, face like an empty box, I'd be in a state, what would I do if I were dragged out on the dance floor? you say you don't want to dance, you don't know how to dance, what's the matter with you? I'm desperate, no, I don't want to go, why do I have to go? if I never used to go to the other parties, my girlfriends didn't even ask me, no, I don't want to go to this party, not this one or any other, I don't know how to dance, my mother's always telling me how I'm clumsy, she's thin but she's not light on her feet, she just clumps around, a sack of potatoes, I don't know how to dance, I can't go to any party in the world, dumb not to know how to dance, but who'd teach me, no, I don't want to learn to dance, I'm not up to learning, I'm so clumsy, heavy-footed, even though I'm thin, a bean-pole, she doesn't know how to dance, I don't want to go to any party in the world, never, you hear? never, you stop that now, you have to go, it's your father's friend, he works where he does, it won't look right if you don't show up, this girl is getting to be a handful, if I don't want to why are you making me? later, you'll say you don't go out and never get to go anywhere, that's enough said now, be quiet, you've said too much already, you have to go to the birthday party, if you don't know how to dance, don't dance, I felt so dumb, I'd go, I'll go, I'm going, I went, heavy with shame, lead feet, chained down in I don't know what corners, the music, this child is thirteen today but she's already a grown girl, she looks like Lana Turner, doesn't she? the music playing, change the record, put on a rumba now, the young girls, the boys, the rumba, her father my father's friend, the father of my little thirteen-year-old friend, looking like Lana Turner, here I'm sixteen, who did I look like? paper doll, face like an empty box, her father my father's friend, my little friend's father takes me by the hand, come dance, my clammy, sweaty hand, come dance, me struck dumb and rooted to the spot, the rumba playing on, my father saying she's bashful, she doesn't know, me struck dumb and rooted to the spot, the hostess' father, nothing would do but I should dance a rumba with him, the rumba is so easy, ta-ta-ta TA, my hand even clammier and sweatier, I don't want to learn, I can't, I, no, the mu-sic, everyone's looking right at us, oh, don't be silly, nobody's look-ing at us, come, come dance, come on, I don't want to, everyone's started to look, I'm way out there on the floor, come on, put that rumba back on again, nothing to it, ta-ta-ta TA, is her father out to make me look ridiculous? some kind of courtesy, there I am scared to death way out on the floor, stiff as a board, like a ton of potatoes, I can feel their eyes going right through me, everybody had stopped dancing, everybody clapping time, ta-ta-ta TA, the rhythm knocking everyone out, I no longer myself, riveted by so many prying eyes, the clapping, just what did I think I was doing out there? where's my father, I want to go, didn't I tell you I didn't want to come? I can't take the first little step, the hostess' father pulls me, by force? gently? I'm face down on the floor, the laughter, the screams, the howls, wall of thorns, but what on earth did I do? my father embarrassed, I must learn to dance, voices and more voices, yells, mirrors broken, breaking in my hands, there I am dancing among broken mirrors, the laughs, titters, the squeaks, the rats running up my legs, my feet gnawed away, how can you dance with your feet gnawed away? with all these rats around? only who is that laughing? my sons behind the mirrors, their faces twisted out of shape with laughter, all because I don't know how to dance disco, my sons told me not to dance in front of their friends, my father called me on the carpet for making such a mess of it, paper doll, face like an empty box, I didn't want to learn to dance because it's sinful, a man and woman together, embracing, my sons are right to be laughing, I'm no age to be wriggling around to this crazy music, my husband never in his wildest dreams could he see me disco dancing, there comes my husband, laughing, why? he says for me to look out, he's not about to keep an old woman around, what's he laughing at? can he have seen me dancing disco? how funny, me doing my bumps and grinds, what bumps and grinds, I'm just trying not to fall down, the broken mirrors cut my feet, my little brother wants me to show him how to dance, is he crying or laughing? how can anybody not know how to dance? how can you dance with your feet gnawed away? the laughter is multiplied in the glass of the mirrors, the noise of the laughter grows in the midst of the sound of mirrors shattering, how many rats are there, counting the images? and without the images? the noise of the rain on the pointy shards, the rain wetting my feet, my heavy feet, the rain flooding the intersections, the white rainwater eating away the street corners, rivulets setting my body free, my face in rain, my hands in water, my feet lightly floating in the rain.

8

The woman who writes me despises my passivity. For me, saying yes is a way of saying no. When I affirm myself, I'm denying her. No matter how much she has denied me, she can't escape my power. She's my prisoner, even when she's not putting me on paper. I make demands on her, because I force her to look at what she likes to think she's forgotten. I open up her wound. Not to get even but to survive. I keep her dangling, since she doesn't know, and never will, how to develop what I give her page by page, syllable by syllable. She thinks she knows how to read and write, when really she can hardly spell me. She writes only when I want her to. Like now. She wants what I want. Even when she's not thinking about me. She doesn't know she loves me in the midst of her hate. When she denies me, she's affirming me to the fullest. My slender schoolgirl body, bones showing, suddenly fleshing out, curving in here, thrusting out there, soft curves the mirror revealed to me. Suddenly, why I don't know, someone said to me, girl, you're lovely. Without smiling or bursting out laughing. Just joking? Pretty, the mirror repeated back to me. The strange sensation of knowing I was the object of certain glances that sent a shiver down my spine. My father frowned, just where do you think you're going? I never went anywhere I couldn't tell him. When I would run into someone who liked books, I always had plenty to chat about. Eighteen years old. It was scary. Looking out the window of my room, I could see new stars in the sky. The far-off beat of ritual drums in the dark night. The son of the cook at the house next door had gone into military service. When he would hear the beating of the distant drums, he would keep time with his feet, throwing his hands up high. What beating was this brought by the wind in the deep night flooded with stars? The vast black night submerged in sounds and perfumes and drops of light. Looking out the window, I would breathe in the warm scent of the mango tree in the yard. The green scent of mangoes cradled among its branches. An unfamiliar thrill running up and down my body, you have a very pretty body, blushing with embarrassment, I didn't like to get compliments from boys. Or did I? A nice feeling of not being a stiff paper doll. She really is a doll. Boys would look at me. The thrill down my spine. My father didn't want me to use lipstick. And I didn't.

One day you took advantage of the fact your father had gone to bed, his eyes were bothering him, his room dark, the house silent, everybody walking around on tiptoe. You were about to leave. A mere movie you got to go to from time to time. You were going with a girlfriend, you had on your new dress, your hair done nicely, after you'd rolled it up and then brushed it out to look pretty, and, at the last moment, you'd decided to put on a bit of lipstick you'd sneaked off and bought. No, you wouldn't do that. The lipstick had been given you by your aunt for your eighteenth birthday. At that time every eighteen-year-old girl wore lipstick. You looked at yourself closely in the mirror, your red mouth, you thought you looked pretty. You went to say good-bye to your father. Yes, as soon as the show was over you would come straight home. After all, your father was sick and you were going out anyway. At six-thirty you would be back, he needn't worry. The room was dark, he hadn't seen that you had on lipstick, remember? Then your brother, who was not going to the movies with you, said, daddy, she has on lipstick. Do you remember? Your father ordered the windows opened, what's going on? Your mother stepped back. Your father grabbed a face towel near the bed, a rough one, and started rubbing your mouth, rubbing and rubbing, very angry, saying that no daughter of his was going out on the street that way, you stood your ground and turned more of your face toward him to be manhandled, until it started to bleed, and he saying, isn't that what you want? There you are, as red as you please, red all over.

It wasn't quite like that. He took the lipstick off my mouth, but he didn't make it bleed on purpose. My father was the son of a powerful landowner from the interior, used to ordering people around, whip and spur at the ready, and he was by training and temperament a man who knew how to make himself obeyed. My father pretty much kept to my grandfather's dogmatic ways. A woman painted up that way is a prostitute. My mother never used the least bit of color on her face. Why should things be different for me? I'd stepped over the line. My father's anger. My own remorse, repentance, shame for having tried to take advantage of the situation, the darkened room.

You almost went to pieces as if you had committed a crime. Your fear, imagining that your father might die because of you, his being ill and needing complete rest, and you taking advantage of the situation. About all you could have done, since you lacked the courage to confront him and do what you wanted to. You never forgave yourself for having deceived your father. You wept all night long for fear your father might die. You went every ten minutes to his door, to see if he was snoring. If he had died, you had it all planned. You would kill yourself. You couldn't live with your remorse.

The woman who writes me confuses her emotions with mine. The one who went to the door of my father's room, to find out if he was still breathing or had died, was herself. After she had declared for freedom. She disobeyed all his orders, but kept on feeling guilty. At a time when young women had a set time to be back home at night and didn't go out alone without saying where they were going, she, the woman who writes me, never bothered to follow those rules. She never set a time to be back home or said where she was going or with whom. But when she did come back, if father wasn't awake to complain and make a fuss, she would go directly to the door of his room, to see whether he was snoring. If he had died, she too would have died. She had it all planned. She would kill herself. She couldn't live with her remorse.

You wanted your father to die, to get rid of that pressure. It was only natural. To think that he would die was the same as desiring his death. Don't you see?

I loved my father very, very much. I gave up everything out of love for my father. Why would I want him to die?

You hated him. No one loves anyone who mutilates anyone else's capacity for love. The gift of loving was amputated, severed from you. You came to grips with yourself through hatred.

My cuts, my scratches, my lacerations. My acts of love. My deeds, my misdeeds. All for love.

There you go again with your niceties, your blindfolded eyes. Hate is a part of men's and women's love. A ferocious hate, which few will admit exists, underlies all relationships. Why deny it? Love is bounded by hate.

The woman who writes me is incapable of a pure sweet thought, unencumbered by revolt. Sacrifice lies exactly in the middle, between love and hate. Between free choice and imposition. To me, what difference does it make if I use lipstick or not? It never mattered. What bothered me was provoking my father's anger. He would be beside himself. I would be consumed with fear and remorse, when I recognized my guilt. What hurts most is guilt. Sacrifice freely accepted and chosen turns into joy. The joy of loving.

Guilt hurts when it exists. Your guilt is to feel guilty without being guilty. You run away from reality because you lack the courage to face up to the truth.

How do we know what's true and what's not? Which is truer? To paint your mouth with lipstick or leave it its natural color? Which is truer, to force a situation and make your own wishes prevail, or to give up one's desire, in order to avoid a clash? What's so absolute about our desires? Rouge on one's face, a ring with a blue stone, a piece of chocolate, a street corner conversation, a boat ride, a favorite record, a bedside book, a fashionable dress, the vulnerability of a plunging neckline, a ripe fruit, a flower in a vase. What difference does it make in the universal order of things? To put lipstick on one's mouth or not to? To put a flower in a vase or not to? For your husband to come home at seven in the evening or at nine o'clock or after midnight? Whether he likes a lot of seasoning or a little? Whether your son goes out on a motorcycle or in a car? What difference does a broken doll make in the life of a young girl like me? Is it so important to know what part of the chicken eggs come out of? It's all the same if you're a stiff paper doll or the prettiest girl on the street. If my son lives by night, at times, who cares, it's all the same. If he likes beer better than orange juice, nothing changes in the natural order of things. To speak softly or shout, study or play the guitar, go to school or to a bar. If the rats start to gnaw at my feet the first thing at night or toward the end, the stars won't change course over something like that. Not over anything in the world. The rats will come in any case, no matter whether it's a lot of them. They'll come. And every night they'll gnaw at my feet. Which is truer, a live rat or a tiny elephant broken in pieces? A gnawed-on foot or a doll with no face? China dolls' faces were painted pink and red. Red on the cheeks and mouth. Red on the mouth. Like lipstick. A lipstick that won't come off when a person rubs it. It breaks but it won't come off. That's why my brother broke my doll and she had no face. I have many faces. I walk with my head down so no one can see my wrinkles. Wrinkles look like rat tracks. Better not to have a face, like my broken doll. My husband wouldn't keep track of the rat tracks on my face. The rat tracks show time plowing away. Time bleeding away. Furrows and signs. No use painting your face, to pretend. What difference can an old face make in the earth's turning? Or in the course of the stars? Which is truer, a young face or a face gnawed at by time? To use lipstick or not to use lipstick, it's really not important. I don't use lipstick. My father didn't like it, my husband doesn't like it, my sons, what difference can it make if my sons think my mentality is colonial, or even medieval? Would the rats stop gnawing at my feet if I used lipstick?

The first boyfriend I ever had, I didn't have. The first thing he asked me was why I didn't wear lipstick? Is it so you can kiss? I was eighteen, he was too. He used to ride his bicycle in front of my house, I'd be on the veranda, pretending I didn't see him, the book in my hands, my eyes on the page not really on the page, he'd come back, I'd pretend not to see him, one day he spoke to me at the streetcar stop, outside school, you're very pretty, why don't you go to the beach? I didn't explain that my father wouldn't let me, didn't explain that my father thinks it's indecent for girls to go walking by the Barra Lighthouse, the boys standing along the edge of the sidewalk, watching the girls go by, the sort of thing my father wouldn't allow. I couldn't tell him about it. Nothing I could say, I said nothing, tongue-tied, afraid to ask him if he liked to read, I didn't want to say anything stupid. At times I used to think it would be nice to have a boyfriend. My father says no. How do you converse with a boyfriend? What do you say and what do you not say? But think of the novels I'd read. The adventures, the episodes, love affairs and non-love affairs. Not understanding much and not knowing I didn't understand. For some time the boy on the bicycle kept passing in front of my house, I'd be on the veranda, the book in my hands, I'd pretend to be reading and not to be watching the street. I could meet him outside school. But what would I talk to him about? I didn't know how to ride a bicycle, I didn't know if he liked to read. Once I went to the movies with a girlfriend. When the seat next to mine was left empty, I saw that he was the one who sat down beside me. Was I pleased? or wasn't I? First thing, he rested his foot against mine. I shifted over. Then he leaned his shoulder into mine. I shrank back. Did I like it? or didn't I? Then he held my hand. I pulled my hand back, a shiver running down my spine. The second time he held my hand, I let him. The shiver ran right through me, the strangest feeling, my hand a frightened bird between the boy's two hands, with the lights out no one saw my face, red with embarrassment and plea-sure. A deep sense of guilt at that inaugural moment was boring into me. When he put his arm around my shoulders, my body went stiff, defenseless, unresisting, everything hap-pening at once, he was kissing me on the face, then aiming for my mouth, my mouth without any lipstick, red and quiv-ering, unsure how to respond to his quick light kiss. Then passionately, his breath coming short, he tried to take my mouth into his. Helpless, for a moment I let myself be elec-trified, but so scared that I got up, went running out by my-self, so scared, but what had I done then? What sort of a per-son was I? How could I let myself be swept away like that? How could I look my father in the eye? What had I done then? A streetwalker, that's what I was. But what was a streetwalker? My mother saw me come in, only she didn't notice how scared I was. I tried to talk to her, she gave me a little smile. I went up to my room, didn't come down for dinner, made up a headache. Would I tell my father? Telling my mother wouldn't do any good. No, better my old nanna. What if I worked up my nerve and told my father? No one had seen anything, not even my girlfriend, I think, saw the time he kissed me, no one knew anything. It was all over so fast. Seconds. No one saw. Truly. But the consequences? I washed my mouth over and over. When I left the movie house, I couldn't stop spitting. As soon as I got home, I ran up to the bathroom and stuck my finger down my throat to vomit. I vomited a lot, perhaps that way I'd be free of troubles, who knows? How could I be sure? As for telling my father, no, not on your life, I wouldn't have the courage. He'd kill me or throw me out of the house. But what about my old nanna? I went down to her empty little room. Emptiness of days forever gone. I picked up and hugged the medals that were lying on the table. I couldn't ever do anything like that to my father. He'd die of shame. I went back to washing my mouth out over and over. At times I thought I'd managed to get rid of my troubles, other times, not. With all the unwed mothers there were, it couldn't be that simple. The greatest despair of my life, for me to be pregnant, my stomach swelling, no way for me to hide it from my father, him beating me and kicking me out of the house. My father dying of embarrassment because of me. Streetwalker. That night, no thought of sleep for me, bitten by the rats. I wanted to get up and go to the bathroom to wash my mouth out again, but my feet were gone. The rats came and gnawed at my mouth, gnawed at my lips, gnawed at my tongue. I woke up in a fever, resolved to measure my stomach every day. If it started growing, I'd kill myself. This decision gave me some peace of mind. I didn't go down for breakfast, I stayed in my room, lying down, dozing off and then waking up with a start, observing my stomach, reassuring myself with the solution I'd come up with. After I didn't show up for school, my girlfriend came by my house, on the way home from school. She wanted to know what had happened to make me go running out that way. Adding that when she saw he had sat down next to me, she turned away from us. He was awfully close, she didn't want to be in the way. As soon as I left, he left too and that was the last she knew of it. So what had happened? I started to cry. My girlfriend got more and more curious. I asked her, do you think a boy of eighteen can make a baby? My girlfriend's mouth, red with lipstick, flew open, her eyes opened wide. How far had I gone with him? Sick with shame and worry, I confessed that he had kissed me on the mouth. At the movie house. As long as I live, I'll never forget the way she burst out laughing. I hear and I'll always hear that laugh, its echo piercing the eardrums of my memory. The uneasiness, the sense of ridicule that covered-uncovered me. Wall of thorns. For months afterwards, my girlfriends at school would laugh and ask me, just when is it your baby is due? I had no idea which was more excruciating, my girl-friends' making fun or the fear that my father would find out the truth. If he ever did, I'd kill myself.

9

When I was very small, I wasn't afraid of rats. I didn't even know what rats were. The rats came later. When I was very small, my little brother wasn't yet born. I reigned supreme in my home. My home. My father. My mother. My nanna. The things that I had were just plain mine. The only one who broke my things was me. It's true that my father had wanted a boy when I was born, instead of a girl.

This was your first feeling of guilt. Because you started out as a disappointment to your father, you've always tried, and gotten nowhere, to make it up to him. From then on, you set out on your path of submission and obedience.

When I was very small, I had the run of my father's lap. My mother's lap was mine. I didn't share my nanna's lap with anyone. Wide open, with no divisions or boundaries. The yard too was wide open. And free. The only thing was I couldn't go near the cistern. The water was dirty and deep, its walls down below caked with mud. Voices from the neighbors' yards mingled with other familiar sounds, dogs barking, chickens scratching, wind in the leaves of the mango tree, birds being birds, the swish of broad papaya leaves, dripping faucet, clothes soaking in a tub full of suds. Late in the afternoon, sometimes, I walked down the sidewalk with my father, holding his hand tight. Other times, I'd sit, my little wicker chair, in front of the main gate. Nanna never left me. There was a streetcar stop right in front of the gate. The streetcar came from Amaralina. Right in front of my gate, the black Bahian woman would come by, her full skirt, lace blouse, a tray of African fried beans on her head. A tray on her head, the coconut candy woman would come by, wrapped up in her green shawl, her feet spreading wide in sandals. The fishermen would come along barefoot from the beach, straw hats on their heads, carrying wicker baskets. Where's my little red fish? My nanna would let me ask them. I wanted to give a coconut candy to the black boy, son of the cook at the house next door. My nanna wouldn't let me. He'd go by, dancing a little shuffle, drumming on a box, his head shaved clean. At night I'd see my nanna hand a little package of coconut sweets, across the garden wall, to the black boy's mother. My nanna would come back to the house, with a nervous tinkling of medals. It's time for bed, angel. Go get your daddy's blessing, and mommy's. Off in the distance, the loud beat of drums cutting through the night, heavy with stars. Don't count the stars if you don't want a wart to grow on your little finger. The headlights got ahold of the reflections of the window panes and dragged them across the wall of my room. My nanna, sitting at the foot of my bed, prayed with me. My nanna told me stories about good little girls who turned into princesses. My nanna's hand on my face was nice and warm in its roughness. The loud drums cut through the deep dark night. The tall drums of Xangô. My nanna used to tell me. Staring out into the black night. Who is Xangô? Sleep, angel child, sleep. When there was an entertainment in the main square, my father let me go with my nanna. She'd buy a numbered card for me at the charity raffle. Once I won a little elephant. The day my brother was born I gave the little elephant to him. When they had the Mother of Waters festival, my father wouldn't let me go to the beach with my nanna. Right in front of the gate, I could see the black Bahian women going by, all in white, starched petticoats, necklaces of many-colored beads, on their heads shawls wound into turbans. They carried flowers and presents. Why? My nanna watched, her gaze lost out across the sea waves. Who is Yemanjá? Who is Oxum? Come in the house, angel. But my nanna couldn't tear herself away from the gate, her gaze lost out across the sea waves.

My father's friends would say how smart I was. Pretty little girl. Except that I soon got unpretty thanks to the teenage beanpole look. My father was proud that I had learned to read so early. My father's friends were surprised. My father's lap was nice and big. I was happy when I heard the news that I was going to get a little brother. But I cried if they told me I'd need to move over and make room. The way they said it. Move over. I saw I'd move over right up against the wall. There I'd be in a high chair, couldn't get down by myself, in a huge corner of an empty room, walls stretching out. There I'd be, shunted off to one side. When my little brother was born, nanna, who was my nanna, came to be my brother's nanna. There she was, burning lavender, the smoke spinning out through the whole house, the thick fragrance working into the skin of the day. They pushed away my bed, which used to be next to my parents' bed. They moved me out to the far end of the room.

That was the start of your expulsion. From their room and their laps. You wanted to kill your brother.

I used not to worry about it, because I was sure I didn't have the courage to throw my brother into the cistern. One day, I don't know how, there I was, way out back, at the edge of the cistern, looking at him, drowned with all his ribbons and embroidery, floating in the dirty water, ribbons and embroidery bobbing all around him, his little eyes closed, me watching from up above, he down below. I knew that if I grabbed my father's fishing pole, I could push my brother's little body down under the water and nobody would ever again tell me I was too big to sit on my mother's lap. But if I was big, why didn't I take my little brother in my lap instead of pushing him into the cistern? So tiny and all alone down there in the dark and deep. I was crying out loud, my parents bending over my bed asking me what was the matter, my mother wiping away my tears with her gentle smile, my father lifting me into his lap, be careful not to wake up your little brother. I looked over at him asleep in all his blue ribbons and embroidery, boys' color. What's the matter? I didn't answer, crying more and more, looking at my brother. My father said I'd had a dream, I shouldn't be afraid. If he'd known what I was dreaming. My father put me back to bed again, he'd be just a little ways away. Don't cry anymore so you won't wake your brother up.

Your bed off in one corner of the room. That was the last time you ever saw a lap. To punish yourself for your desire to drown your brother, you threw your ring down in the cistern.

I didn't throw my ring down in the well. It fell in by accident. It slipped out of my hand and rolled in. Maybe it didn't even fall into the well.

You know it fell in. You didn't have the courage to throw it in yourself, afraid your father would get after you. You found a way. Play like you were rolling the ring, on the edge of the cistern.

That's not how it was. The woman who writes me twists the story all around. Muddy water gives a crooked reflection. Clear running water washes clean the earth and the sunflowers. The mind of the woman who writes me is all slimy and dirty, a dark cistern feeding on what it destroys. She knows so little about anything that I can keep her in suspense. Since she writes me, she always has the idea that she can express her opinions. She doesn't know what's going to happen at the end of this page. She doesn't know what the next sentence will be. She's so silly she imagined she was imagining me. That is, she thought at a certain moment in the text I would get my feet on the ground. I wouldn't have the strength to resist the pressures and I'd leave home. Exactly what she did when she was in her early twenties. She just leapt to the conclusion that I'd be all set to leave home in my late forties. If I ever did leave home, it would be so heavy a move, I couldn't take it. My submission is built in by now. I don't get my stability from being a rebel. I live to get along with others. I live my days giving in here and there, it all builds up for all time, one layer on top of another.

From the moment you dreamt that you drowned your brother in the cistern in your yard, you started discounting your feelings of guilt and remorse. Being off in one corner of the bedroom didn't seem unfair to you any longer. You tried to get rid of the one who took your place. We always want to kill those who take what's ours.

I never wanted to kill anyone.

Every day you kill the one who kills you. Your husband and your sons, in the very same way you decided to kill your brother and you killed your father.

I never wanted to kill anyone.

You just didn't want to; if you wanted something, you got it. That's how the rats came. They gnaw at your feet every night. More than once you've drowned in the cistern in your backyard. That filthy water. Right now you want to kill the woman who writes you.

This is my story. She has no right to go adding herself in. She simply has to go the way I set it up.

But here you are, setting up your own death wishes.

She always misinterprets my moves. I neither wanted to kill nor have I killed. Furthermore, to want to kill and to kill are not the same thing. Or are they? I wanted so badly to kill myself and, meanwhile, here I am, alive.

You're dead. A long, long time ago you drowned in the cistern. You threw yourself in along with your ring.

I have other outlets for my feelings of guilt, my remorse, other ways to add them up. My guilt, my remorse. Not liking my husband's being so fat.

Because you hate your husband so much, you kill him every day. With guilt and remorse gnawing away at you, you're willing to share your bed. The same way you just went along, went off to a corner of your parents' room, the same way you gave up on the lap that was also yours, now you're sharing your marriage bed. You allow your husband to bring a woman who works for the company into your room, into your bed. You go out shopping, pretending you believe they're going to work on urgent business. You're always having to punish yourself because you never think you've been accommodating enough. You condemn yourself, because you know you hate your husband. His being so fat is just the surface part of a whole pattern that you hate and pretend to accept. You think you should not take a stand, not even in your heart, when your husband, at the dinner hour, takes out his dentures to pick bits of food that got stuck or are bothering him. You have made yourself accept things that go against your grain. For you it's not enough to be revolted seeing the dentures on top of the table, that mass of half-chewed food stuck in between the false teeth. You have to find a way to punish yourself for your disgust, the same as you punish yourself to this very day for what you consider your childhood crimes. You spend your life flagellating yourself twenty-four hours a day. Before, secretly, by throwing into the cistern the toys you liked best. Or even by eating bitter jiló fruit, which turns your stomach, just to keep your husband company at dinner. Ever since your marriage, you pretend not to care about his ridiculous affairs, with that crazed need of his to show what a man he is, bragging about his manly vigor and an organ a bit more developed than normal, his pride and joy, trying to spread the idea that any woman lucky enough to experience such gigantic size is in for a rare and unforgettable treat. You pretend not to notice when he goes limp and can't perform. You pretend you don't notice that his

friends snicker at his vaunted virility. You don't even know
how to hide your shame and embarrassment when, in that
leering way of his, he pats you on the butt and tells anyone
around, here's the lucky lady who can vouch from personal
experience.

When I was little, I used to like to watch the storms come in.
The air heavy with thunder. The sky crisscrossed with lightning. Nanna was very scared, Santa Barbara. I wasn't brave
enough to laugh at her fears, the way she'd kiss her medals
and cover up all the mirrors in the house, I hope she forgets
and leaves one uncovered. My nanna. The black boy, son
of the cook at the house next door, jumping and dancing
around in the rain. He was king of the lightning.

When I was little, my nanna used to take me wading in the
ocean. The wave would come in and flow out, to the delicate
sound of bubbling foam breaking around my feet. A wet
sheen on the wet sand under my wet feet. My feet washed in
the clear seawater. The water would be covered with light.
My feet were set aglow, strange and swift. My feet were
edged in water and light.

$\boxed{10}$

Ever since I was a little girl, I've liked reading immensely.
My poets, my novelists. My open space of freedom and fan-
tasy. My time for privacy and unwinding. When I read, I cut
all bonds and break through my limitations. I crystallize
other worlds, conquer the phantoms. I gather forces to survive. I smooth away sharp edges and screams. When I read, I
read. What I've gleaned from other harvests I bring home for
seed. I gather and regather the fruits of other flights and
other walks, the flowers of remote and unique travels. My
arms filled to overflowing, I lay the words down in gestures
no one sees. I keep them and move on, in search of new
risks. I prefer to read when I'm alone at home. My husband
and my sons don't understand my revitalizing tears of emo-
tion, my laughter or my smile of complicity. They make fun,

put me down, wall of thorns. The spell is broken. My father would react differently, when he found I'd been carried away by some story with a sad ending. We can't have all this soft-heartedness and blubbering. Once it took a whipping to make me stop crying inconsolably over the black doll that fell out of my window on top of the vegetable man's wares. The more I was punished to put a stop to such foolishness, the more I cried. I couldn't control myself. Oh, Master, sir, for the love of God, the medals keep tinkling.

Early on I learned to contain my emotions. My extroversion is channeled into introversion. I can explode in front of my mirrors. But always when I'm alone. The colors of my clothes are as restrained as my gestures. I had no choice but to contain myself. They made me—I made myself. My armor. My security blanket. My defense and survival. My wisdom and my strength. My father didn't care for a lot of laughing. At times, if my brother and I laughed too loudly, or a bit too long, we were ordered to stop. Often it was really hard to, because the more my father ordered us to stop, the more we felt like laughing. Getting a whipping was almost always the only way to make us stop laughing. Oh Missy, don't let him, do something.

The one who got whipped the most was you, because you were older and had to be an example, remember? You had to hold yourself in, even your cough. In the first place, you must not catch cold to avoid causing extra work or worry and giving your cold to your brother. And especially because your cough didn't let your father get his proper sleep. You suffered most when you got whooping cough. Your father often thought you were coughing on purpose. The rats ran around your room and gnawed at your feet. One night your mother went to your room and found you were cold and purple, trying to keep from coughing, your pillow over your mouth. And there was your fear of rats. Your mother started crying. Your father gave you a glass of water, but he didn't take you to sleep in their room.

I think it's good to keep your feelings in check. Cool and understated. I'm the result of a long, patient apprenticeship.

Mind and body find composure, just a little moderation holds them in place. I cut down on conflicts in everyday matters. I avoid clashing over extremes. I shrink back and trim my sails. I drink a glass of warm milk every night. When my father died, I acted calm and collected. In the days following, I exceeded no one in tears and lamentations. To be sure, I needed to weep. But I was careful and held it in. It wouldn't be right to sadden the atmosphere, whether tears, or sighs. I think it's good to hold your emotions in check.

I really like to be alone in my room. I don't live in the place I'm in. I live in my corner of the bedroom, among my belongings, things in my personal care. My leather armchair, my floor lamp, my Byzantine Madonna on the wall. A little bookcase of favorite books. My ceramic pieces. My blue vase, invariably with its white rose. My little begonia plant. The photo of my First Communion. An older photo, in my angel costume. The iron that belonged to my nanna, who only liked a coal-iron. My nanna's medals, fastened to a heavy silver chain that I at times hang around my neck. A few *mil-reis* coins from the time I was a child. My father's silver inkstand that had belonged to my grandfather. My records. My record-player. A tiny box with souvenirs of my First Communion, all the little saints that had been given me since childhood. An album with family photos, from our days in Rio Vermelho. A fashion magazine I replace from time to time. A newspaper clipping of a Vietnamese child, a famine victim. My old collection of Eucalyptol soap pictures. A magazine clipping, with an erotic pose. An old calendar. A mirror. A lady's fan. These things are always there-here, inside me. Other things come and go. When I shut myself in my room, I shut myself inside my things, my belongings, things in my personal care, my notebooks of poetry and stories, the sketch of a novel, a few thoughts, no diary, I threw it away. Among my things, I'm really me. My space and my time, with no ruler and no clock. Inner time frames of infinite extension. My chance to be free, when I am free. Near the window that opens to what is closed in. And I remain suspended where I live.

11

You saw it with your own eyes. She just won't accept me. The woman who writes me. She avoids me, runs away, and she's back. She thinks she can forget all about me. She hasn't so much as touched my-her story for over two months. It's true that she didn't lack for reasons. I recognize she has many demands upon her time, even with the crazy way she lives, she doesn't schedule things, never has to do this or that. She doesn't wear a watch. Thinking that she can just sort of set her own time. Just another of her illusions. No matter how much I want to bring her back to reality, she's too stubborn to see, she keeps thinking she's in control of what she does and wants. Actually, I depend on her to come into the picture through this writing. If she doesn't want me to, I don't come into being. That is, if I want her not to want to. Yes or no, stay or go. A black-and-white choice. She never gets out of my control. She went for over two months without writing me, but she didn't get away from me. She always depends on me to say yes. Her way is to say no. I'm the voice of her guilt. She pretends I'm not talking straight to her innermost self. She's still hoping to be rid of me. All she does is strangle me. She doesn't kill me. If she kills me, she'll die, too. Without my feet, gnawed away at by rats, she cannot walk. She needs my feet to feed the rats that grow in the underground burrows of her veins. I keep quiet so she won't have to scream. I fall down so she can keep on walking. I wiped the smile off my face so she could let out her nervous laughter. My sacrifice doesn't come out of any desire to help her. Now I'm alive, I have to fight to exist. And to exist, I depend on her. To take my own measure. Every life is measured in the struggle to cover-uncover guilt. I'm the voice of guilt that she's unwilling to hear. How she hated me. How she wanted to get out of writing me. She was so tied to me, and went two months without writing me. She had her reasons. She needed to put the finishing touches on the stories that were just about to go to press. She doesn't know her characters only exist because of me. She thinks she created them. The woman who writes me is the creature of guilt and remorse. She was born out of my obsession. These two months she hasn't been writing me, she's been living, living me. Day after day. Hour after hour of lost sleep. I run clear through her. She went over her stories. Her stories rooted in guilt. Afterward she went on a trip. A film festival. A while back she made a short film. The woman who writes me doesn't want to write me any more. But there she is, in spite of herself, sitting in front of her machine, I get to say what she wants. I know the exact moment to step in. To make my moves, and she can like it or not. She won't kill me. She doesn't want to die. Tied in with me, bound to my yes, woven into the fiction of my wishes.

We need to keep it straight who's character, narrator, and author. I'm the character here. The narrator is herself, the woman who writes me. The author has nothing to do with the story. The authoress, that is. These are three entities which, as it so happens, have come together. Here, the narrator, that is, the woman who writes me, is a character of the character. My character. Which doesn't cancel out the basic difference. As I've often said, she's who she is, I'm who I am. As for the authoress, I don't know who she is. She doesn't come into the story. Or does she? Could we be projections of her fantasies? It doesn't make any difference. One thing is certain. When the author comes into the novel, he becomes a character. Turns himself into fiction. In this book, she, the authoress, would be a character of my character. And so, a creation three times removed. I guarantee the authoress wouldn't willingly take on a role in this story. She has her own views about her autonomy. But she doesn't take part in this story because I don't want her to. If I wanted her to, she'd take part. Try as she might not to. I'm not interested in her lack of interest in her life. If I depend on the woman who writes me, the authoress depends on me. Without me, this book won't be. Without the woman who writes me, I won't take shape. And the authoress won't exist, without one and the other. Each level has to interconnect. Everything depends on everything.

I depend on my husband. My husband depends on me,

however much he considers himself the big strong man. I depend on his dependency. I used to depend on my father. And my father depended on me. Author of my days as he was, still he depended on me. There I was, a poor creature down at his feet. The ones who give the orders depending on the ones who obey. Who bears more responsibility? My father lived by taking charge of things. Of people, above all. Dominating. Domination, dominus, absolute master. Took up crown and scepter every day. It revitalized him. He existed. My house was run by royal fiat. Hardly ever did anyone dare defy the iron rule. One day, the discovery of my diary, totally out of line. At age seventeen, the need to write down certain impressions. At that time, I gave my pillow the name Johnny. Johnny was my faithful friend, there to calm my tears, my crying jags that used to come over me for no reason. My diary was called Franky. Johnny and Franky, there for me to lean on. Real human beings. At that time, I'd read a famous author's thoughts on the lack of understanding. I think it was Goethe. He spoke of the impossibility of people's understanding each other completely, gestures and words don't come across the way they're meant, at any rate, that was Goethe's idea. No one understands anyone. I used to go around saying that. My father told me to stop that nonsense. The biggest piece of nonsense I ever said back then was that parents should understand their children. That really set my father off. Where did you ever get such an asinine notion? Don't let me catch you saying that again. Children are the ones who have to understand their parents. The way he turned it around later came to make sense, to seem inevitable. Someone will have to understand someone. When parents don't understand their children, it's up to the children to understand their parents. If not, the family falls apart. Suddenly, I began to understand my parents, and from there it was just a step to accepting them. But at seventeen I wasn't exactly there yet. At seventeen, I still really needed to be understood. Despite my superhuman efforts to accept. To accept despite not understanding. Hence, Franky. Hence, Johnny. Keeping me company in my desert loneliness, my own wasteland. My dear Franky. How good to have you.

How good to have Johnny. I just lay my head on Johnny's shoulder and forget all my troubles. When I hold Johnny tight, the world is like a golden dream. I love to give myself to you, my darling Franky. You're the only ones who understand me, who stay with me weathering the storms. You're the nectar for me, I'm the little bee that can't get enough, eager to feed in the garden of life. In the garden of life I'm a tiny rosebud. Every night Johnny comes to drink in the sweet rose of my dreams. Every night I give Johnny my rosebud that opens up for him, for him alone and no one else. For him alone, no. I also give myself to you, my darling Franky. I open up only to you two. You're my blue skies after my storm. Last night I held onto Johnny and before I realized it, I was covering you with kisses and tears, Johnny dear. I love you both, my dearest Franky and Johnny. I belong to you both. You light up my darkness. I feel loved by you both and only by you both. Only you can love me, knowing that I'm not a virgin. I didn't know what virginity meant. I thought being a virgin meant being good like the Virgin Mary. In my mind, virginity stood for goodness, humility, gentleness, selflessness. I didn't think I could come close to those sentiments, I could never be good.

At seventeen you didn't have the slightest idea what the sex act was. Meanwhile, your sex was there, constantly demanding, even if you didn't know where the drive was. You rubbed up against your pillow, you held it between your legs, you felt the mysterious object that made your sex throb, without a clue what was really happening.

The woman who writes me, just because she's so loose and oversexed, drags my arrested innocence through the muck.

You confuse healthy normality with promiscuity and depravity. You were using your pillow to deal with a young female's first stirrings of sexual desire. Why deny it?

I was a naive lonely little girl, with no one to help me work up my courage to break through my father's prohibitions, with no one to explain to me what words like virginity meant. Never in my life could I have just figured it out for myself. Once, at a little birthday party at my aunt's, somebody asked me what my sign was. Virgo the Virgin. And I said, I don't look like one, do I? Fourteen going on fifteen years old. The way the guests were looking at each other, everyone squirming in their chairs, snickering, wall of thorns, paper doll.

For all your not knowing, you knew. You knew so much that you caught on and you never forgot everyone's laughing right at you. You didn't want to want to know.

At times, I really get impatient with the woman who writes me. We're forces that join only to fall apart. We only come together veering our separate ways. However odd it may sound, I didn't know what virginity meant. In my diary, I wrote down what my sexual ignorance got me into. I'd say things not catching the double-entendre out of sheer ignorance. You all can imagine what a shock I got when I came home from school and found my father beside himself with rage, my diary in one hand, waving his arms, all red, his hair pushed down on his forehead, lined up and down and across with wrinkles. You scum.

His leather belt was shaking in the other hand. Daddy, for the love of God, what was it I did? You tramp, you whore, you bitch. My mother fainted. And on top of it all, look what she does to her mother. The leather tracks on my body beginning to bleed. My screams, my father's screams, the neighbors, the doctor showing up, my father puffing, red in the face, this girl wants to kill her father, but her father is going to kill this tramp, this scum, did I faint? half strangled with fear, oh my God, I don't want daddy to die, if he dies, I'll kill myself, what was it I did? our neighbor the doctor running around, helping my father, helping my mother, holding my hand, calm down, later he'd explain everything to me, explain what? he wanted to treat me, saying he'd already explained everything to my father, explained what? he's giving me medicine, after you've finished, you're going to get a good night's sleep, don't cry any more, you need to go out with other girls your own age, he'd talk with my father, no more crying now, put away your diary, I didn't want to, swearing that never again in my life would I keep anything secret from my father, wanting to and not wanting to go to my nanna's room, her already in bed, I came in sobbing, throwing myself down beside her, the icy roughness of her hand on my face, hugging her, burrowing into her silent medals, I'm standing up looking her in the eyes, her tears running down, I'm holding her hand very tight, passing my hand over her crinkled gray hair, the icy and sweaty roughness of her hand on my face, yes, I'll get some sleep, I never, never again wanted to keep a diary, I shouldn't have hidden my diary, what had I done that for? my diary was hidden in my dresser drawer where I kept my panties and my bras, I didn't want anyone to read it, it was my diary, all mine, it kept me company in my lonely times, then and there I tore it up, no, never again, throw this pillow away, for the love of God, Doctor, I'll never keep things secret again, no, it's no use, Doctor, your saying I didn't do anything wrong, I hid my diary away from my father, that's not what he's upset about, he thought you meant something else by what you wrote, meant what? oh my God, what did I do? Doctor, if my father dies, I'll kill myself, Doctor, is my father better? there was nothing wrong with him? you're telling me the truth? yes, I'll get some sleep, I'm so sleepy, one day my sons found one of my notebooks where I write things, no one ever reads what I write, I write only for myself, one day one of the notebooks got into the hands of one of the boys, they all saw it, they all read it, even the boys' friends, at first my husband thought it was funny, then he got offended, he doesn't like my keeping anything from him, otherwise he can't trust me, how can he? the boys thinking my writing is funny, wall of thorns, my poems aren't funny, my stories are so sad, just how did it go, momma? some old lady forty-three has a kid? the doorman at her apartment building did it, come on, you can do better than that, mother, he came by to fix the plumbing and fixed her up with a little piece of pipe, wasn't that it? the lady of the house must have been really aching for it, no, the doorman was, her being forty-three and still a virgin and all. You'd have to be some doorman and really hard up to try making it with some bag who in forty-three years never found anyone dumb enough to take her on, mom, do you think Snow White was a virgin? listen, mom, when she went off with the prince, the seven dwarfs had had her, one by one, or all seven at once, right, mother? you could tell the story of Snow White

56

in bed with the seven dwarfs, wall of thorns, Snow White the tramp, Snow White in heat, momma, tell us the story of Snow White, ask your sister, look, momma, she doesn't want to tell stories, bad, bad girl, why don't you want to tell a story to your little brother? you're big, he's little, go tell him a story, go on, once there was a princess who lived in a magic castle, a magic castle where there were no mice or rats, a castle surrounded by a garden with no fences, a garden with no fences and running through it a little stream of clear water, clear water where the princess would come every day to wash her tiny feet, her tiny feet that were never gnawed at by rats, there just weren't any rats, because it was a magic castle and water ran over the princess' feet, where's my diary? Johnny, my love, my darling, kiss me, hold me, Franky, I confess my sins to you, you know, I deceived my father, I do things behind my father's back, in secret, and you're the only one I tell because only you understand me, daddy doesn't understand me, no one understands anyone, goodbye Franky, goodbye Johnny, I won't have you any more, because of me daddy almost died, forgive me daddy, forgive me Johnny, forgive me Franky, I'll never break another rule, take it, daddy, you can tear up my diary, you can burn my pillow, good-bye Johnny, good-bye Franky, no, not by fire, I'd rather throw myself in the water, I want the water on my feet, my feet the rats gnawed on, I'm going to tell you a story, sweet little brother, once there was a nice little girl, a very nice girl who turned into a princess, a princess who lived in a magic castle, a magic castle where there were no rats.

12

This morning I had to go to Rio Vermelho. I went by the house where I was born and grew up, where I spent my childhood, my adolescence, my early young adult years. I gaze at my old house, today almost in ruins. I'd be lying if I said I wasn't touched. I feel a knot in my throat, gooseflesh, take a deep breath and try to get over the feeling I'm going to vomit. To me it's funny to hear people talk about their nostalgia for the past. Why nostalgia? Is it that days already lived are any less sad than those right now? People romanticize their childhood as if their days of innocence necessarily coincided with the happiest of times. It's not true. No party, no picnic. Childhood is the time of fear. Of getting really scared. Terror. Why nostalgia then? When I was a child, I hadn't learned yet what can lead to a more suitable life, better for one's own self. A willingness to give things up. Although my present life is anything but a bed of roses, it's on an incomparably more regular course than before.

When you were little, you still reacted to things. At least a little. Today you don't react any more. Paralyzed, apathetic, alienated, indifferent.

I'm patient. Being soft but ready to act. I give consent if I'm given consent, I can be patient about accepting people, including the woman who writes me. When I was little, I still hadn't developed very much patience, and I paid for it more than once. Hence the intense fear and panic I felt, that came from my not being able to adjust to my father's temperament. By giving up the things I want, I can live the life I want. Not a bad way to cut down on walls. At peace with my husband and sons.

What you call peace is your ability to efface yourself.

The woman who writes me is continually getting into fights because of her egotism, her vanity. She's always insisted on having her own way, whatever the cost. Little by little I stopped making decisions about things. I want what my husband wants. Being soft but ready to act. So simple. There are the windows of my former house. If my father wouldn't let me stand at the window watching the street and the people going by, often I'd start crying, and get punished for it. If I had spontaneously given up my window, I wouldn't have suffered the fear of punishment or felt so terribly sorry. The windows of my former house are shut up. The last owners had just sold it to a construction company. Before long, an apartment building will be put up. The windows are shut up. The gate is locked. The house is almost in ruins. But it was a lovely house. The walls are caked with dirt, weeds grow where the garden used to be. Through that gate, I went forth to get married. Through that gate, my father's burial procession went forth. Behind that grating, I knew my first fears. I was afraid the dog would get in. I was afraid of getting to school late. I was afraid my china doll would get broken. I was afraid ants would eat up the guava bush. I was afraid my father would get after me if I spoke to the black boy, son of the cook at the house next door. I was afraid of not doing my school work the right way. My father didn't allow low grades. I was studying at a school run by nuns. I dressed up like an angel and walked in a procession, along with other girls, a long white dress of shiny satin, wings attached at the back, a silvery star on top of my head. Moments of supreme joy. The greatest punishment for the little girls at school was not to dress up like angels in the procession or at celebrations in the chapel. My greatest fear at that time was not being able to dress up like an angel. My greatest dream, to crown Our Lady. A dream merely dreamed, that's all. I was a good student, with good deportment, at the end of each month I got a special red ribbon, which Mother Superior awarded, a little ceremony after recess. Once I didn't get the special red ribbon. A certain morning, a girl from the fourth grade came into my first grade room. She asked the Sister to send a girl to her classroom. What for? To give them the correct answer. I was immediately chosen. I always knew things. The Sister wanted to know what had happened in the other classroom. They were saying a boat was a place where you put water. Any girl knows what a boat is. Boat? I didn't know what a boat was. Then say right then and there I didn't know? Anyhow, I was already on my feet, ready to leave. Better tell them I didn't know in the big girls' room. In my room, everybody was used to the idea I knew things. At that point, I heard one girl say to another, a boat is a little ship. Now I knew what boat was. The girl who knew ought to be the one to go. Too late. I was on my way to the fourth grade classroom. I mustn't tell a lie. If I didn't know, I would have to say I didn't know. I don't know. The Sister in the fourth grade was very serious, the entire class bursting out laughing. Wall of thorns. Silence, But daddy, if I didn't know, I couldn't say I knew. But you did know. You heard the girl say a boat was a little ship. You acted like a fool. I couldn't understand my father's anger. I told him what happened, sure he would praise me. I'd told the truth. My father very angry, you're a big fool. I didn't get punished at home, but I was dying for fear Sister wouldn't let me dress up like an angel at the next festivity. I've never been so afraid of anything in my life. They took away my red ribbon, but on the next Sunday there I was parading around Saint Anne's parish church, one of a group of little angels with clasped hands and piously contrite gazes. It was forbidden to smile, it was forbidden to look to either side, it was forbidden to talk. I followed the rules to the letter, which was easy for me, and I was rewarded with that supreme bliss. To dress up like an angel. I savored those blessed moments until the day I felt the worst shame ever. During the procession I broke out in a cold sweat. My feelings got the better of me whenever I went out as an angel. Long beforehand, my excitement grew, I wouldn't eat or, if I did, ate in a hurry, without chewing properly. That day I had an upset stomach. I broke out in a cold sweat. My stomach churning. It's forbidden to look to either side. It's forbidden to talk. The procession was making its way slowly, from Mariquita Square, then around Saint Anne's parish church square. I felt like vomiting. It's forbidden to look to either side. It's forbidden to talk. Without turning my head, and with my eyes less piously contrite, I looked for the Sister. I couldn't vomit. It was forbidden. An angel doesn't vomit. With clasped hands as always, the cold sweat colder, it's forbidden to turn your head, I started to vomit. The Sister pulled me by the arm. I looked toward her fearfully. She wasn't angry. She seemed to feel sorry for me and handed me to a woman accompanying us who sewed clothes for the poor children in the school. My angel dress, all covered with drool and bits of unchewed food. The sour smell was unbearable. The last time I ever marched as an angel. For my father there was no reason to get all that excited over just marching in a procession in a white dress. No reason at all. It might not be at all good for the child. And anyhow, another dress would have to be made for her, this one is ruined, all stained with vomit. You see what happens to little girls who disobey? You knew you were supposed to chew your food thoroughly. For several days, I was unable to keep any food down. I had the feeling I was vomiting up my own flesh. No, I don't miss my childhood. Nor even the greatest happiness of my life, to go out dressed as an angel, my hands clasped together, my eyes piously contrite, not smiling, not looking to either side, not talking for whatever reason. And naturally not vomiting. I always used to watch the procession go by. My nanna's hand held mine intensely. The little girls dressed up like angels, long white dresses of shiny satin, their wings attached at the back, a silvery star on top of their heads. My nanna's big roomy hand. I didn't crown Our Lady.

Every time you go past your childhood home, you can't muster any nostalgia for those days. You've only your great urge to vomit. And do you know why? Repressed rebelliousness. Nausea over a family structure completely insensitive to your small desires, your minuscule dreams.

I hate feeling sorry for myself. And I hate it when other people feel sorry for me. Each of us has his own life. I may choose, I may lose. I don't want compassion from the woman who writes me. Pity is a form of scorn. I know I have the strength to face dangers. The strong don't weep. They vomit.

Yes, you vomit, when you find the weight unbearable. How many times didn't you vomit from your bedroom window all over the sunflowers your father had planted. How many times didn't you bolt from the table, hiding your queasiness from your husband, food still in his open mouth or fanning his mouth with his hands, to soothe the burning from the pepper he'd put on in gobs. You're ruled by the feeling of nausea.

The woman who writes me has never really learned what love is, a non-resistance yielding to wind and fire, spines and scales, voluntarily. She'll never understand my willingness to give in, to step aside. Being soft but ready to act. No matter how true it is that the digestive apparatus and the nervous system are related, it's also true I've always had a sensitive stomach, touchy digestion. And if my digestive troubles are of nervous origin, that doesn't interfere with my sacrifices for love. All love calls for sacrifice. Spines and scales, voluntarily. My nausea is independent of my acts of self-sacrifice.

As soon as you got married, your nausea multiplied. You could barely stand to go to bed with your husband. All the trouble you went to to wipe from your thighs what you thought to yourself was foul-smelling sputum. Always that terrible urge to wash yourself after the sexual act. Your body wants a bath as if you wanted to purify yourself from all that slime and sticky drool that drips out of your husband's mouth when he has an orgasm. You feel so much repugnance that you don't even notice your husband seeks you out less and less. For you it seems like a rest, a relief, but the fact of it is he's more distant and away from home more. You insist on not noticing that it's over between the two of you. After so much giving in and stepping aside, you lost for good what you'd already lost. Furthermore, you lost what you really never had. All in vain. What good was your sacrifice? All the years of exclusive dedication to your family went for nothing, broke down, disintegrated, rotted, don't you want to take a look? You don't look because you don't want to, you prefer to be blind and avoid any sort of truth that might prove what a waste your struggle was, a job fit for Sisyphus, every day a loss. You never paid any attention to the ridiculous posturings of your husband who, from the outset, cultivated a strange mania for passing himself off as some high-powered sexual athlete, with his taste for dredging up imaginary sexual adventures, as if he were the most indefatigable and irresistible virile specimen in the world. Because of your alienation, and for your own convenience, you never even used to think about this barhopping Don Juan's cheap conquests. Even when he was promoted to manager of a big company, he never gave up his mean, vulgar taste for lamebrain women at moderate prices. You really ought to pay attention. You'll find he's been strutting around here lately less than usual. How long has it been since he came home for dinner? Has he ever before slept away from home so many times? How many months has it been since he stopped seeking you out? Because you insist on not understanding what's right before your eyes, you manage to feel better about situations that were becoming more and more intolerable in your physical relationship with your husband. He may care a lot about appearances, but he doesn't have any scruples about going out with a salesgirl from a dress shop. Before, he camouflaged his bargain-basement conquests, pretending they were high-society ladies, whose names he pretended to protect to keep them a deep, dark secret, so as not to compromise anybody. A question of ethics, he'd say, smiling with his false teeth, filthy with food particles. His latest conquest didn't even make it in the try-outs for a second-rate samba group. Not pretty, not young, not good at shaking her hips. And, mostly, lamebrain.

The woman who writes me wants to drive me crazy. Why does she want to tear down the world I've built? This little world made out of wisps of cotton padding, in between the sharp edges of glass and pointed steel. This nausea. Nothing seems able to cure this nausea. The windows of my former house are shut. The gate with its wrought iron grating is shut. Where's that smell coming from? A sour, yellow odor. But I'm not going to vomit, I mustn't get my angel dress dirty.

It's forbidden to talk, it's forbidden to look to either side, it's forbidden to vomit. Angels don't vomit. Angels have wings and fly. Silly, how do you expect to fly with stiff paper wings? Angels don't exist, yes they do, no they don't, they do, I'm not going to crown Our Lady because I'm a bad girl, you vomited all over your father's sunflowers, I'm sorry, daddy, I'll never vomit again, but this sour, yellow smell, I got my dress dirty, my legs are dirty, slimy, what's

happening? where are my mirrors? I don't want to see my face,
what's happening? my legs, please, no, no, not now, what will my
father think of me? but this bitter smell, close the windows, now you
see, no, I'm all dirty, I'll get washed up, I want water, lots of water, I
want to get washed up, in sea water, in river water, I want to drown
in rain water, in flowing water, I want to get washed clean, I want to
drown, the windows of my former house are shut, the gate barred,
the sour yellow smell, where is this smell coming from? from my feet
the rats gnawed at? yes, rats make me sick, very sick, I open my win-
dows, I open my windows out wide, with my wings of stiff paper,
angels don't fly, they fall, I've lost my feet, I've lost my wings, I'm
falling, falling, between sharp edges of glass and points of steel.
Waves of stench. Yes, the woman who writes me is right. I feel such
nausea.

13

At certain times, I get to feeling so tired. Those sleepless
nights wear me out, I'm dead to yet another day. Like a ton of
lead. Depression spreads in gooey trickles all over my arms
and legs, it seals my pores shut and brings my blood to a
standstill. Lethargic, draggy, I'm drained clear down to my
core. My arms hang like stone weights and won't move. My
feet are sunk deep in sleep, never in a thousand years could
they move. A slimy ooze tells me there's no hope of getting
through. I stay on this side, fused into calloused time as it
creeps along. Gnarled. Deep lead. My mind full of cobwebs.
Feelings can't get to me, I don't laugh, don't scream, don't
even hold it in. I unlive. I go against living. What did I do
with my life? What did I do with my death? When was it
I died? How to get away. Slack times leave me the deadest.
Senses can't take in sights, sounds, smells, tastes. Only the
weight on my skin. Things are gross and crude to touch.
And there's nothing to them. Not knowing how to love, not
knowing how to feel, I don't know how to know my face in
the mirror. Anti-face. I uninquire, unattempt. Anti-me. Un-
me. Unmirror.

14

I don't like to admit that all my sacrifice has gone for nothing. I balk at the waste of doing-undoing-redoing everything. How to accept the idea that my husband can leave me? No. Not that disaster, it ending like that. All the years of life together crumbling to bits, swept away. I can't accept that. The wind doesn't blow down the house founded on rock. The woman who's caught my husband's fancy isn't strong enough to destroy our marriage. Built on a firm foundation. I know I'm not in love with this man. Never really loved him. But my struggle to keep the family together. My sons. The young people of today, with their freedom that doesn't free anyone. My sons need a father's presence. Even if my husband doesn't love me, doesn't want me. A father's presence. This woman will be like the others, a big crush, he cools down and breaks it off. That's how it's always gone. The house that weathers the storm. My struggle, my life. My sons' problems. They'll grow out of it. They'll go back to school, good boys, good at heart.

You need to see your sons the way they are. Outlaws, degenerates, addicts, perverts. Not all young people are like them. The oldest was once taken in on a drug charge. The middle one is a homosexual and once tried to bring his young lover to live with him right there at home. The youngest, when he does come home to sleep, shows up so drunk he can hardly find his way to bed and the next morning he turns up sprawled on the floor somewhere. You've got to admit your husband is away more and more of the time to avoid seeing his sons. It's not just because of his affair. Your sons are lost causes. Their father has no moral power over them. Their mother never got them to obey. You look so weak and helpless your sons don't take you seriously. You failed. Your sons are hopeless.

I need to take a good hard straight look at all this. I don't want to be influenced by the woman who writes me. She sees my life from her own warped little outlook. And what if my outlook is skewed too? I wonder where truth is? In my yes? In her no? Not in the yes? Nor in the no? The truth is we never get truth. The endless faces truth wears. Who can recognize the faces of the faces of truth? Ever since I was little, this drive to get at the principle behind things. From down deep, only odd bits and scraps. We never grasp the total pattern. No one gets a hold on all the faces. Our eyes can't see what our eyes can't see. And we see without seeing. We make our way across the outward surface, at times we scrape a little ways down into it, but we hurt our hands, our eyes on fire with the desire to go down deep. Condemned to the surface. Sometimes a gap opens up in the visible and we get a quick flash of the invisible. In the visible, we don't see what we see. In the known, we don't know what we're knowing. Through the empty depths of mirrors, the layer on layer of illusion crusts on. The endless faces of broken mirrors. The glass edges on which we hurt our eyes, eyes on fire.

What's on the other side of the mirrors? What's burning out beyond the images? Can I get a good straight look from inside the whirl of surfaces, the maelstrom of outward appearances? From the inside where the faces come together and break apart? The truth of the truth is, we never will get truth. I see it straight: I never will get a straight look. Not yes nor no nor perhaps.

My sons aren't hopeless. Just going through a difficult phase. Is it my fault if they don't obey? What did I do wrong? I guided and cared for them, gave my all, lived for them. I was always eager to make it up to them for their father's impatience. Lay down the rules, then lay on the leather. You can beat some sense into an animal, so why not a boy? So what could I do but try to tone down such severity? In many ways, my husband is like my father. My father took a liking to him, let him come courting and marry me. The harder my father laid it down, the more I'd give in. My sons, a generation in revolt against the values of the past, being themselves, aren't to be tied down. My sons expect to cut loose, break down the barriers, run out of bounds. Their only law, to follow their own law. How long can that last? It's inevitable they'll begin to see the other side of the boundary line, this side, where the law is the law and rules mean security. Good kids who still need their father and mother together. Even if the father stops speaking to them. My husband holds me to blame for the way the boys have been acting. Just going through a difficult phase. But they're not hopeless. Is it my fault if they don't obey? Where did I go wrong? Am I wrong to sacrifice my life for their well-being? I stopped wanting anything for myself, threw away all my dreams, stepped out of my skin, so I wouldn't get in anybody's way. I got rid of my shadow so I wouldn't be standing in anybody's light. I did without my face, so I wouldn't upstage the faces around me, I bound my hands to keep from getting other people's things, I glued my fingers together to keep from taking hold of anything and calling it my own, I tucked my words away down deep in my throat, so no one would hear from me anything they didn't want to hear, I took up no more space than my slender outline, what did I do that was wrong?

I need a reasonable explanation for people's aggression. To live is to attack and come under attack. Peaceful co-existence only happens when someone submits to what someone else said to. Either we let loose our frustrations against the other person or we let ourselves be beaten down into the ground. Why? Why in any relationship is there always one who walks all over the other, one who gets squashed flat? Why do we repel each other so much, when we need each other to survive? Why do we hate each other so much, when we need love like a vital organ? Can hate be a form of love? Is it because of love that they hate me so much? My husband. My sons. And me? Can it be out of hate that I love my family? What do I feel when I love?

You hate them harder than you ever thought you could hate. Long ago, you got tired of your theory that to live is to learn to understand and accept others. You need to admit what's going on inside you. Why not have the courage to face up to your part in all this? To live is to hate others. Massacre is the way of the world.

I need to get a clear picture, even though I know I never will. Where is the truth that isn't here? Why is it always such a strain to get along with other people? Whether we let the other in or shut him out. Either way we feel bad. No doubt left: happiness has no chance. We can't stand being alone or having other people around.

Until now, you have known being alone while co-existing. Why not try co-existing while being alone? Try to live alone and try for another level of co-existence. Go away. Why not take the plunge? Why not give yourself a fresh start? Go away. Leave your husband. You've taken enough humiliation. You can't do anything more for your sons. It's time to let yourself try a new way of life. Or it will be too late. You think your family can't do without your presence? Your absence will do more good. For yourself and for them. Get brave, change your life. You know how to find work. Go away. Reject being dependent on your husband for survival. Show yourself you can set your own life course. Leave now. Or it will be too late.

I need to get a clear picture, even though I know I never will. The endless faces truth can wear. What does it mean to say yes? What does it mean to say no? Not yes not no not perhaps. What, then? Not the near side, not the far side. Not here, not there. Not before, not after. What is there on the other side of the mirrors? The broken mirrors?

15

Saturday before Carnival. I'm home all alone. What do I care whether it's Carnival or Ash Wednesday? Everyone's gone out, I like to stay home by myself. When I'm by myself with nothing to do, I'm not all alone with nothing to do. I can settle into the space of my space. I leave clocks and dates behind me. I sit down in the corner of my room, close to the little things I like and don't like, my own things, my own possessions, in front of the window that opens onto what's closing in, directions strange to me. I escape to the north, I watch myself going south, I make a new start eastward, I end up heading west. Beginning and end, a new beginning. This window is not the window of my room, in my father's house. It's the window of my corner, in my husband's apartment. This window opens me onto what's closing in. Like the other one. They're the same window. This one, on the seventh floor of an apartment building in the Vitória district. That one, in the townhouse in Rio Vermelho. The sounds have changed, but it's the same crash of things banging into each other, in a time without clocks or dates. Who is that young man? Strands spun out of imagination. He watches me from his window, not far from mine. He smiles at me. I smile back gratefully. Our eyes are arrows meeting. The sweet cool feeling in my belly. The doorbell rings. I'm falling into his arms. He pulls me close in against him. I melt into that embrace, it's then, later, and now all at the same time. No, I can't take my clothes off. Why not, love? Only if you close the window. Close the curtain. This glowing half darkness where nothing matters. This gentle warmth, light slicing through it. Hold me in waves. Kiss me in masses. We're alone, between the stars and the soft fur rug. I feel like an animal in heat. His skin goes clear through my skin. Where did I learn his skin? We're alone, our pores feeling each other out. We shudder dangling over the abyss of my depths that has no beginning or end to it. We break out of the lines that once limited our bodies that are now knowing and deciphering each other. We go beyond mirrors and reflections. Who am I who, from my window, hid myself away from clocks and dates? Who is that young man smiling at me from his window, the pane with its reflections? The strands of imagination. Across from my window in the townhouse, I see the ocean. Down below, the sunflowers my father ordered planted. Outside my window on the seventh floor, the ocean is a patchwork of shimmering blue, beyond the buildings. Deep down below, the sacred mango tree is flowing with life. No matter how old it may or may not be. The tree is ancient. Its branches overhang the street and reach across the years. Between my yard and the yard of the house next door, a mango tree grows in defiance of the wall, jutting out over both sides. From the window of my room I can see the mango tree in the yard. The fragrance of ripe mangoes wafting in. Through which window? Close that window, girl, come inside. I know the young man smiling at me, from behind a pane full of reflections. The strands of imagination spin. He paints a picture that I can't see. What's on the canvas he's painting? He looks at me and smiles. I smile back my thanks. At night, when everyone is asleep, I let my braids run out free and lean out the window. He comes up, lightly, sprightly. Take off your clothes. He wants to paint my portrait, nude. No, I can't take my clothes off. A cold breeze is blowing from off the sea, I can't take off my nightgown. Do you want your portrait painted or not? Shake your braids out free, your silky braids. That's the way. Are you still cold? Your hair covers up your whole body. Don't make a sound. They might hear. He runs his hand through my silky hair. Stroking my face. Stroking down my arm. He wants to kiss me. All right, but not on the mouth. This is going to be the prettiest portrait ever. At the art show they're going to want to know who posed for it. Will you go to the show? Why won't your father let you? The best painter in the whole world. After the show, when he wins the prize, he won't need to climb up my silky braids, dangling down from the window. He'll come in the front gate, newspapers in his hands, and he'll tell my father, here, read it. That's how my father will learn his name. The great painter. My father will be at a loss for words and say, of course, that's right, certainly. And my father won't say anything, when he sees my nude portrait at the art show. If that's what you want, go ahead, marry. It was fate, father, we were made for one another. He can only paint if I pose. Close the window. There's a cold breeze from off the sea. From the window of my father's house, I see the ocean, quiet and blue, I see the shrill yellow sunflowers, I see the swelling curves of the mango tree in the yard, I see the squares of windows of other houses. My house is at the corner with the hill and the street with the streetcar. From my window I see the streetcar going by and stopping. I know the people who pass near my window, the people who are going to take the streetcar, the people in the streetcar. They smile at me. Who is that young man who takes the streetcar every day, the same time every morning, the same time every evening? The strands imagination spins. He looks at me and smiles. I smile back gratefully. A medical student, he passes by, his heavy books in his lap, he only tears his eyes away from his studying when he goes by my window.

He studies a lot, but he finds a way to say he's thinking of me, that I'm the love of his life, I tell him, I can never be your wife, hold on, you'll surely find a nice girl to love you, no, no, I'm the only one for him, if he can't marry me he'll kill himself, I'm the shining star of his life, the sunshine of his life, the light of his life, no, I can't be your wife, but if I don't marry him, he'll kill himself, from my window, I see the funeral procession pass by, between the streetcar tracks, the cortege stops in front of my window, everyone in black, men and women looking at me, was it over her? is that pretty girl the love of his life? the love of his death? they tell me don't be afraid, no one wants to hurt you, they know I'm not to blame, they only want to honor the last wish of a man about to die, he asked that this rose be given to me, this rose that he kissed before dying, and his diary as well, here is the diary, where he wrote everything he felt for you, thank you very much, I accept the rose, but not the diary, I can't, take the diary and cast it into the sea, but what about his wish? his wish is that my wish be honored, I said, my father won't allow diaries in the house, but the bottom of the sea is the only tomb worthy of a love story, from my window I see the ship passing over the horizon, I wonder where it's bound? where is it coming from? after this horizon, opposite another window, in another city, where a girl in a townhouse watches and asks where is this ship coming from? is it bringing someone's lover home? yes, it's bringing someone who loves me and won't be satisfied just to watch me at a distance, from the window, he wants my lips, but I tell him I can't, why can't you, love? The strands of imagination spin. Why don't you bear the sign of destiny? What sign? the ring, what ring? the ring that I threw down the cistern, you know, in the cistern in my yard where the sand is loose, always shifting, the ring worked down into that sand and out to the seashore, whoever finds my ring will be my lord and master, along every seashore in Bahia, he swears to go forth questing for my ring, I'll only marry the one who finds my ring, my destiny, and my sign, if I ever break my vow, a fate worse than death will come down upon us, farewell, you haven't found my ring, he will sally forth in quest, take a ship that will bear him where he must go, perhaps my ring has come to rest on the sands of Africa, farewell, dear heart, on that ship goes the man who loves me, from my window I'll see when he returns, manning an enormous caravelle with blue sails, who knows when? I'll be waiting in my window, close the window, girl, there's a cold wind from off the sea, a wind out of Africa, a wind that tousles my hair and gives me goose bumps, the strands imagination spins, from my window I see the black boy, son of the cook at the house next door, he's sucking on a mango on top of the wall, sitting there watching me, he smiles at me, I smile back gratefully, he's the prince of a warrior tribe that came from Nigeria, his ancestors traveled to the coasts of Bahia in a slave ship and lost their kingdom and lost their power, but the princely heir is biding his time and will return and will reclaim his birthright, he wants me to help him free his people, he wants me to be proclaimed princess of the tribe, he tells me the story of his people on the slave ship, it was like a dream of Dante's Inferno, the decks scarlet in the lanterns' glow, bathed in flowing blood, the clank of irons, crack of whips, legions of mankind, black as the night, oh why? Lord God of the oppressed, banish this pennant from the seas, when he grows up, he'll leave for Africa, he knows how to dance his royal dance, he smiles at me, the mango, his white teeth, I smile, I don't know if my father will consent to my leaving for Africa, especially to marry a black man, but surely if I'm going to be a princess, my father will allow it, I'm afraid I'll never get used to living in such a hot place, even as a princess, I smile at the black boy, son of the cook at the house next door, he's sitting on the wall of the backyard, he looks at me, offers me a ripe mango, I close the window, girl, come do your schoolwork, what year was slavery abolished? that fisherman is the grandson of a slave, chief of the sister tribe to the black boy's tribe, the son of the cook at the house next door, the black vendor woman is so old that she remembers the stories in the slave quarters, except she doesn't know she belongs to a royal family and *she's the aunt of the cook at the house next door, the king of lightning is an African king, royal dancer, kingly smile, but if my nanna still lived in Africa, she would be the queen of the tribe of the black boy sitting on top of the wall, sucking on a mango, smiling at me, I smile back gratefully, black men are strong and I think they're scary, I see black men going through their fancy* capoeira *moves, underneath the ancient mango tree, their muscles bulging in time with the melody, their whole bodies moving to the sound of the twanging steel string, something is moving beyond the bodies, above the play of light and shadow, the delicate leaves with green light shining clear through, the fragrance of ripe fruit, who's that man standing under the sacred mango tree? The strands imagination spins. He looks up, he looks at me steadily, he smiles, I don't recognize him, but I smile back gratefully, he keeps looking at me amid the green reflections of the ancient shadows, who am I that I don't recognize myself in his gaze or in his smile? he comes inside the building, rings the bell, he came to paint my portrait, he's spent years trying to find where I moved to, he never painted again, never had any more shows, never could after that, love, you cut off your silky braids, why? he was sad to see my long hair gone, now he can kiss me, kiss me on the mouth, come, take off your clothes, I take off my clothes, the sweet cool feeling in my belly, why did we separate? you were my destiny, my life, he spent all those years dreaming of my mouth he'd never kissed, ripe mango all soft inside, all of me nestling in his mouth, in his arms, I've waited so long for you, all those years he spent waiting for me, love, the hand of time hasn't touched your body, waiting for this moment to arrive, the colors of the mango faithfully reflect the many hues of day, he says to me, all soft and juicy inside, eager, hungry, he plunges in, he leaps up over my dark and unfathomable colors, love, we're alone, between the ancient mango tree and the soft fur rug beneath us. We're alone, our pores feeling one another out. We shiver suspended above the abyss of my depths that has no beginning or end. We break out of the lines that once limited our bodies that are knowing and deciphering each other. We go beyond mirrors and reflections. Who am I, the one who from my window hid myself from clocks and dates? he never forgot me, in the window of my room, smiling, smiling once more, looking, looking back, long braids streaming out in the sea wind, he wanted so* much to paint my portrait, now he'll never let me go, I am his destiny, his life, I close the window, I'm at home alone, looking out my window, night is falling amid the last reflections of the sun on the panes of other windows of other buildings, mirrors making up their own red suns, here at the window where night is falling far from the violence of clocks and dates, my window above the sacred mango tree, who am I, the one who hid away from the hours and the years? who am I here at the window, unable to see things as they are, does my window open onto what has been closed for all time? mirror in the dark, with its memory of images that never knew the light.

16

Mardi Gras, I'm still all alone, no one home, would I be any less alone if someone were home? coming up to my apartment, the voices from the Avenue, groups of carnival-goers singing as they go by, the frenzied music of the sound truck, and what if I were to go and have a look around? to listen up close? why not? and what if I put a mask on? I wouldn't be recognized among the crowd jammed into Campo Grande square, would I be any less alone than here? all by my lonesome, what harm could there be in just going down? I'd put on the mask, no one would know me, my face sad behind the mask, I see myself in the mirror, my face a sad mask half hiding, half revealing my deep down unhappiness, why didn't I ever go to a carnival party? why didn't I ever wear a costume? when I was little, from the window of my house, I'd watch people going by wearing masks, a falsetto voice asking me did I know who they are, did I? I'd back away scared, gathering in my big rolls of streamers, someone squirting me with an ether spray that sent chills down my neck, my father's warm hand suddenly lay on my shoulder, turning me back toward the house, it's your brother's bedtime and he won't go to sleep unless you're around, there I was, making a paper mask, two holes where the eyes go, one for the mouth, you know who I am? you know who I am? now don't you cry, baby, don't you cry, it's just me, I'm sorry, Daddy, I didn't mean to scare him, I was only playing, Daddy, all right, Daddy, just at the window, let me stand at the window, Daddy, I promise I'll never scare little brother again, cross my heart, from our yard I could hear the noise of music, voices, drumming, all mixed together with the barking of the neighborhood dogs, the chirping of crickets in the grass, the wind in the leaves, who knows who's behind the masks? who knows my face behind my face? what face is that, hiding on the far side of the lighted mirrors? what face is this, stranded out on this side of the extinguished mirrors? I'm going down there, a mask on the mask of my face, a loose dress like a shroud, am I going? am I not? why didn't I ever go? why not go? the crowd jammed into Campo Grande Square, the reek of sweat and urine and ether spray, the delirious beat of the sound truck gets me moving with the crowd, people in motion but standing in one place, a man's arm around my waist, I resist, but I can't pull away, waves of humanity, I should never have come, take your mask off, let's see your face, who are you? who am I? how did I get into this tangled mass of people? the clinging alcohol smell, the arm around my waist, I try to get away, my feet go up and down in the same spot, I try to squirm free, that arm around my waist, sweaty bodies brushing up against me, stench of sweat, of urine, of alcohol, of ether spray, how can I get away? the dense crowd, harder and harder to get through, now slowly moving forward, under the spell of the beat from the sound truck, I break out in a cold sweat, my whole body shaking with horror, no use screaming for help, who would hear? what good would it do? sheer panic, I'm scared, I want to go home, I should never have come, why did I? I had no idea, it's crazy, my mind is going, I'm going to die, my smiling mask is covering up cold sweat, covering up tears that are burning, burning, I want to go home, how do I get back? and when? the mass delirium with everybody jumping around and shouting, their sweaty bodies all around my body that's shaking all over, the huge, gaping mouths, the drool, the teeth, the crooked teeth, the fillings, the bad breath, the booze smell, the slithering slick tongues, the spit, no one knows who I am, does anyone know who I am? I take off my mask with its built-in smile, don't you know who I am? I scream, I yell, you don't know who I am, my brother smiling, it's him all right, up on the sound truck, don't you know who I am? he's all smiles, his huge gaping mouth, blue carnival snakes streaming all around him, his nightshirt billowing out big, flashing blue trimmings, don't you know who I am? the tambourine in his hand, singing screaming smiling laughing he doesn't know who I am, at the intersection near Fort São Pedro, not so many huge mouths for a *while, the crowd thins out, I go down to the Gamboa district, I want to get back to my house, my room, my own corner, all by my lonesome, who am I under the mask of my face? Me, the one who doesn't want to see the mirror's mark on my face, where's the face I'm looking for, at home alone, I don't even try out the mask that has no smile, there's no one around, no one saw me go out, no one saw me come back, I don't have anybody to tell that I made my way back, the next morning, Ash Wednesday, I put on a little smile, a rigid mask, I set the table for breakfast, I wait for them to wake up, they're taking a long time, I wait, they're not coming, there's no one in any of the bedrooms, the woman who writes me, wearing her Jacu Marching Society costume, looks at me, her mask in her hand, looking tired, very tired, but it's not the tired that comes from having fun at carnival, the woman who writes me looks at me, her mask in her hand, looking, looking at me. In the silence of the mirrors.*

17

For months now the woman who writes me has refused to write me. She's been living me harder than ever before. The way we're living each other is a closeknit thing. We're knitting in tight, right through each other. The passage of time has put an edge on her remorse, has made my sense of guilt sharper. The sense of having lived in vain. The effort to keep the family together. The resounding failure. My husband, since carnival, hasn't come back home. My oldest son has been admitted to a clinic, after refusing treatment for his habit. My middle son was arrested and faces trial for trying to murder a friend, out of jealousy. The youngest one spends his days and nights in a drunken stupor. What about me? Day after day I've thought back over my fiasco. Is it my fault? Am I free of blame? I did what I could. I sacrificed my life and my death, I offered my feet to the rats, I turned both cheeks to be slapped, I buried my face behind the mirrors. Water can't wash away my shame, rinse my skin free of all the filth, freshen my stinking bones. I retch with nausea. Nausea at myself. At the world. The world stinks of rats. I spit in front of my image in the mirror. I spit on my face. What face? The woman who writes me hardly writes me. She can't say a thing. She tried and tried to convince me I had failed, my life was in ruins. The moment I let myself be convinced, she, the woman who writes me, won't be so high and mighty. She'll go right down with me. I want her to speak. She won't open her mouth. Anyhow, what could she say to me? She too can see her failure. As resounding as mine. She doesn't know what to do with her freedom and her loneliness. Her independence, her liberalism, her free spiritedness all came to nothing, since there was never anything there. She was fed up with everything. She always tried to shock me, make me see what stupidity I'd always been bogged down in. Now, for different reasons, we're stuck in the same mud. The very same stench. Total nausea. I look in the crossed mirrors and I don't see her, shoulders drooping, face sagging. Who's that with her shoulders drooping and her face sagging? Before, her cheerful cynical face would smile at me, inviting me to break taboos. Not long ago, she was beckoning to me, all smiles, how I shouldn't just keep muddling along stupidly, I could still have my fling, I was so well preserved despite everything, time was wasting, if my husband didn't appreciate me, I knew very well I could interest an intelligent man, some of my husband's friends gave me knowing looks, why not grab this chance to forget all about my flabby husband? My slender body, thrown away and wasted on the cold walls of the mirrors. Why not seize the moment? I wasn't going to. I'd never done it. Why not do it? Now it's too late, I'm worn out, I let the chance to get even pass me by. They've gone away. I'm alone. I'm old. I'm ugly. I don't look at the mirrors crisscrossing any more. She doesn't look at me, she doesn't see me. She hates me, she does, the woman who writes me. She won't forgive me for failing. She can't see any reason for it, she's still tangled in the same stinking web, caked with the same vomit. These months were worth something for taking stock. For me, for her. My slavery, useless. Her freedom, also useless. Nothing led to anything. The mirrors are more and more being cleared of images. Useless reflections that go skimming coldly over the smooth glass, vacuously. Nothing led to anything. Clots of vomit spot our dresses and impregnate us with a sour smell. The windows are sealed. Hammered down tight. This total nausea is too much for me. Mental and physical asphyxiation. My whole body needs the wind. The wind from off the sea. I open the window slowly. I peer down into the depths of the ancient mango tree. The ripe fruit left to rot on the branches. Right in front of the nests. You're not allowed to climb up in the sacred mango tree. You're not allowed to climb up on the wall that separates the two yards. You're not allowed to pick ripe mangoes. The black boy, son of the cook at the house next door, would climb up on the wall and pick ripe mangoes. One day I climbed up on the wall. Nanna didn't say anything to my father. She cleaned the whitewash from the wall off my knees and my shoes. One day I talked to the black boy, son of the cook at the house next door. Nanna didn't say anything to my father. Her medals tinkled with a worried sound. The wind from off the sea getting all twisted up in my hair. Why can't I climb up on the wall? Why can't I pick mangoes? Why can't I talk to the black boy, son of the cook at the house next door? The medals sighing underneath the starched white dress. Why? Nanna's roomy hand. Its nice warm roughness against my face. No, I won't come down off the wall. I won't come down because I don't want to. Here I am shut up in my apartment, because that's what I want. I won't come down because I don't want to. When I make up my mind to, I'll come down, I'll take the elevator, I'll come down and go out. It's enough for me to want to. But do what, once I'm down there on the street? Do what, shut up in this apartment? Do what, shut up in the little attic room? The attic with the rats. Yes, the attic with the rats. The rats that used to gnaw at my feet. I open the window and see the ancient mango tree. I open the window and see my father's sunflowers. I see the mango tree over the two yards. If I want to, I'll go up on the wall. My father said there weren't any rats in the attic. I made it all up about the rats that came and gnawed at my feet, my real ones. My make-believe ones. When my toes were gone, I couldn't walk. I open the window. You have to open windows. Wide,

wide, wide. I open the window and see the sacred mango tree. I open the window and see my father's sunflowers. I look down at the ground. And if I jump, I'll get wedged in between the branches of the ancient mango tree and no one will see me. I'll rot there. I'll just rot away. They'll never see me, but they'll get a whiff of something rotten. I open the window and see my father's sunflowers. And if I jump. I'll crush and destroy my father's sunflowers. Maybe I won't die. The yellow petals of the sunflowers. The ripe-sounding flesh of the ancient mango trees. Maybe I won't die. The mango tree. The roots aren't afraid of the dark earth. The mango trees. If the rats gnaw away the mango's roots, it will fall down in the middle of the street, all its leaves and nests swishing down. Maybe I won't die. I open the window because I don't want to die of suffocation. Cracks opening up in the great unbroken slab of the day. Light rays shooting through the gaps where it comes together. The ritual drums sounding out their rhythmic beat in the creases that the wind furrows into the cloak of day. Mystery from out of the wind, the wind from off the sea, the sea from a distant African coast. Near, very near, the aroma of ripe mango takes on body, soaks down into my pores now. Above the ancient mango tree, the shining sky arches cleanly overhead. The day pours itself out in brightness across the backyards. Light sparkles on the street of the sacred mango tree.

18

Once more the woman who writes me wants to stop writing me. All tied up in knots. But she'll have to write me, because that's what I invented her for. With power I have as a character of fiction. The main character. The heroine, that's who I am. The heroine of an ordinary failure, of a nameless suffering, of hopeless misery that can't be helped. The woman who writes me, besides writing me, is my antagonist. All tied up in knots, till she can't even give me an answer. My authoress asks me, what now? My authoress wants to give me up. I'm not giving her up. I'm her essence and her cutting edge. Her destiny, driving her on. No turning back with me. I was born flesh and wind. I can die, not go backward. My way doesn't make things easier, it makes things harder. I shape, mold, texture, but never set free. I subjugate and possess. With my deceptive fragility.

My authoress peers at me in fear and exhaustion. She wonders how I'll go about it now, to break through the impasse. I might choose suicide, since my whole world has crumbled. Energy to rebuild another one like it I simply don't have. And I don't want it. I'm not interested in restoring what's already past. No, I didn't choose suicide. Not for me and not for the woman who writes me. Not for the authoress either. I'll find another way.

I open out my mirrors. Inside them, in the depths of the cold surface, a worried-looking figure slinks into view, her face stony, her shoulders drooping, hands hanging limp, knees apart, trying to steady herself. I look deliberately at her feet. They haven't been gnawed at by rats. They're all there. Yes, all there. I place my feet, all there, side by side. Definitely all there. I throw back my shoulders and, with my shoulders, my head. I glimpse the play of a smile around my sagging face. No, not sagging. The wrinkles are fading and show the faint trace of a smile that grows and deepens into laughter. I'm laughing. Uncontrollably. Laughing. A strange smile, that goes to the heart. I undress. Long pants slip down over my feet, all there. I take my blouse off. I'm naked. Solidly at ease with myself, naked in front of myself. In front of my exposed mirrors, opening up the orientation of my body. I feel the cool thrill in my sex with a shiver running clear up to my quivering nostrils. Naked in front of my mirrors. But why didn't I ever do that before? Naked, stark naked, absolutely naked, with no fear, with no fake modesty. It's me, me over and over and over again, comes the unending cry of the images looking out in all directions.

My body stock still in front of my trembling body. It's not a young body, but I can see it's a pretty body, soft curves, firm flesh, shameless. I walk up to one mirror. The tips of my breasts recoil at the touch of that smooth chill surface. I move away and back, and away and back. Again away. To bring my body completely up against my body, I turn my head to one side and press up against the mirror. It's a clammy, uncomfortable chill. To regain the orientation of my body, I step away once more. A warm feeling of freedom runs through my images. I touch my breasts, I touch my sex. Alive with desire. A lewd smile surprises my face in the mirror. I cut off my smile. I look closely. I smile my lewd smile again and I realize it's me. No, it's not the woman who writes me, when she'd sometimes beckon to me and get me flustered. It's me, nobody else but me, not afraid and not surprised. Surprise and fear, right now, are for the woman who writes me to feel. She's literally scared. All along she's been waiting for me to do something drastic, trying to provoke me, daring me, making fun of me for being so shy, so unsure and here she was so open-minded, nothing could shock her. She always did try to shock me, she just had to try out all the pleasures. So, now, just when she's discovered her quest is useless, I've decided to leave. After her downfall and mine. After my despair and hers. I'll have something pleasant to look forward to. My feet are all there and I can walk right over the rats. The woman who writes me wants me around now, so she won't feel lonely. If we weighed our hatreds we'd know just how lonely we really are. I don't want to. It's too late. When I needed her, all I got was scorn and ridicule, sarcastic laughter, abuse. Wall of thorns. I plunge into the solitude of my mirrors and invent my body, folded back into space, rescued in time. A lovely body not young, ready to claim its birthright of pleasure. My hands stroke my body, from top to bottom. They stop at my neck and fluff out my hair to make it fall free, on my shoulders. My hands, circling around my breasts, gently reach the erect tips, they've only known the fat sweaty hands of one man. I can feel the pleasure awaiting my lonely breasts. My hands run on down to my waist, to my buttocks, sink into my sex, ripe humid flesh cradled away from soarings and divings. Now, ready at last for the soarings and divings?

Yes, it's really me, in front of my mirrors that add my selves up and bring them into alignment. But they don't blend me together. The woman who writes me drags herself to the typewriter and looks down at her feet. All gnawed away at. She made fun of my rats and now there they are, my rats, gnawing at her feet. She's frightened, very frightened. I smile and beckon to her, pointing to the attic. She no doubt remembers the walls with no mirrors, the blind walls, the walls that were nothing but walls. Her guilt awaits her. As for me, I take one more look into my reflected look and ask myself. Is it false? The mirror smiles back at me through my mouth.

I step out of the mirrors looking for the fur rug. I lie down on the floor and my pores come to know the bristly softness of the hairs. The wind from off the sea brings me the smell of ripe mangoes. I curl up, I stretch out, I roll.

The reflecting mirrors are empty.

19

The days go by slowly, lazily. Where to begin? Between the wanting to and the doing, the enigma comes out of the gap. What's the first step? If I don't yet know, my authoress doesn't know either. Much less, the woman who writes me. To a certain extent, we know what I'm going to do, but we don't know how, since we need at least a minimum of coherence and believability. My authoress isn't any more credible or coherent than I am. Once more my authoress is giving in to me, anxious to get out of my grasp, sorry she ever listened to me. As long as I don't hand my story over to her, my slender story of subjection and revolt, she, my authoress, will be left with the disagreeable sensation of not knowing how to bring the job she has underway to a successful finish. I feel nothing for her, I neither approve of nor disapprove of her anxiety, I won't lift a finger for her. We're simply restricted to each other. Without love, without hate, in a kind of differentiated indifference that binds us and sets us apart. We're aware of our ties, of our mutual dependence for survival.

I also invent my authoress, to the extent that I give form to her feelings and emotions, to her experiences and the lack of them. Meanwhile, as I've said, my authoress can't enter these pages invented by me. If she did, she'd lose her status as a person, and end up in the position of a character. The life of the character is freer, since it's not subject to the rules of social convention. No, my authoress doesn't have the airiness of a character, she's tied to her codes and would never do what I'm going to do in the pages to come. Also, that's exactly why I'm going to have to take the road you're about to see. No, my authoress doesn't deserve life in the imaginary realm, tied as she is to her banal reality.

I'm going to come back down to earth. From now on I'm going to be free of any sort of preconception. I need to enjoy the life I've been banished from. I'm going to continue creating my reality of independence in the same way I invented my submission.

Even in the freedom of creation, it's not easy to take the first step. Besides, my authoress is hesitating and her hesitation bothers me as much as my decision to subvert the rule that was keeping me in place embarrasses her.

Where to begin? For a week I've said I'll get started tomorrow. But where? Why can't I make full use of the freedom I could get from my privileged situation as a character? On the level of imagination, possibilities are infinitely, irresistibly multiplied. Then what's stopping me? I refuse to consider myself tied to a total psychological coherence and I proclaim the union of opposites. Although the union of opposites can't be said to be illogical. Reality is the sum total of opposites. My timidity developed to rein in my aggression, my docility hid my cruel, aggressive impulses, my prejudices sought to stifle an exaggerated free-wheeling outlook tending toward immodesty. I repress all the opposites that have characterized me thus far. I'm dying to see myself dragged into their wild, fierce maelstrom, and I couldn't care less what comes of my legitimate self interest, more than justified by too much selflessness in the past. Selflessness that wasn't selflessness. It was fear.

Where shall I begin. By putting on one of my sophisticated, provocative gowns? Or preferably my blue jeans? Which of my few friends and acquaintances should I look up first? Should I get a job? It's true that I don't have to work to live, and I don't need my husband's support either, thanks to my inheritance from my father. What color should I dye my hair? Which perfume should I use? What kind of flower should I place in my vase? What color beads for my necklace? In front of my mirrors, I know how to take command of situations. Away from my images, I lose direction and courage. I open up my mirrors. I look for my face. The telephone rings.

Besides being a friend of my husband, he had a way of looking at me that always bothered me, made me look away in embarrassment. He wants to know how I am, if I need anything. Tonight he'll come to bring me the life insurance brochures and forms. I'd never thought about life insurance.

20

I'm ready. But what if he doesn't come? I'd never thought about life insurance. My new perfume is strong and not subtle. I open the window and see the fronds of the sacred mango tree, its fruit with their moist, ripe pulp, cradled in the warm night. What if he doesn't come? The wind from off the sea brings the scent of ripe fruit. The distant ritual drums drive into the black night. What if he doesn't come? The wind from off the sea brings the scent of ripe fruit. The distant ritual drums drive into the black night. What if he doesn't come? The doorbell rings. I dash over. But I don't open the door immediately. The mirror guarantees me once more I'm in good shape. Good evening. He almost didn't know me. His surprise. The way my hair's done. The provocative dress. His hard eyes boring down into me. I hold his eyes in mine. I return his smile with a movement of curves. I take the forms. I read-don't read the brochures. Life insurance. To me it seems funny. What for? I don't take out any insurance. I'm sure of my new smile. The joy of smiling without timidity. My easy gesture. My eye catching his. How different I am. I'm just the reverse. I'm at the antipodes of myself. I'm my image in the mirror. I'm the other. I am I. How different you are. He doesn't know that my yes and my no aren't parts of a whole. They're the same. I am the same. Despite the other I. You look different. I smile, I look in his eye. Don't talk to me about life insurance. Life insurance is death insurance. I'm living. How pretty you look. You're like a different person. Will you have a whiskey? He prefers champagne for a toast to the new woman I am. Beautiful. Beautiful? Music? What sort of music would you like? Yes, of course, why not dance? A firm body holds me gently and gently envelops me, gently draws me near. The firm body of a man pressed to my thin body, the rippling rhythm of the music and my blood, our throbbings joined, our breath one breath, you say you're all alone here at home?

A joy I never suspected could exist, the complete joy of being a woman and feeling desired, the absolutely total surrender to a man whose body is firm, not sweaty, doesn't drip saliva at the climax. The discovery of pleasure. Natural pleasure. The pleasure of pleasure. Like healthy animals, without inhibitions, without subterfuge. A man and a woman beside the rustling of the ancient mango tree, far removed from the sunflowers in the yard at my father's house. Could there even have been sunflowers around my window? I've forgotten the placid sunflower faces, responsive to the breeze and to the light, tossing their little suns and their seeds, under the window of that shy, reserved girl. Engraved in my memory, the moist, ripe pulp of the mango, offered across backyard fences, perpetuated in the ancient tree that rustles outside my seventh-story window, today. Today, precisely today. What do I care for these sunflower petals and seeds blown along by the wind? Ripe fruit hang among the rustling leaves and the nests, here, today. Despite the wind. The wind from off the sea.

I open the window and let the wind run through my hair, loose. I lower my head even more, at the whim of the wind from off the sea. I open my blouse and let the wind from off the sea into my most secret pores. The thrill of pleasure, of full entitlement to pleasure, the skin's pleasure. Without the skin's horizontal pleasure, it would be impossible to plunge into the pleasure of silent, inscrutable movements up and down the vertical. My husband used to coat my skin with sour sweat. The wind from off the sea, clean and fragrant, plunges into my most secret pores. The doorbell rings. My skin is ready, under my half-buttoned blouse, as I go to the door.

Are you alone? Are you sure one of your kids isn't going to suddenly show up? What if he did? He'd see a man and a woman. Don't be so jumpy, you silly man, I'm alone, splendidly alone with you. I smile, looking him straight in the eye. Why talk? Our feelings are enough. Exactly. My skin, invaded by the wind, the scent of ripe fruit. Why on the fur rug? No, don't turn off the light. Leave it on low. How pretty you are making love. Why talk? Are our feelings enough? The taste of ripe fruit. There. How pretty you are, after making love. Yes, put your blouse on. There. Don't button it all the way up.

I open the window and let the wind from off the sea into my most secret pores. The wind that brings to my body the scent of mangoes lost among the rustling leaves and nests. My body, under the folds of my open robe.

The woman who writes me, burdened with guilt, now suddenly she's scurrying about trying to patch things over, so now she seems to be some kind of Puritan, forgetting all about the beliefs that until just now she went through life flaunting. As for the authoress, though she may call herself liberal, she's worried about toning down my outbursts, with mincing words, soft pedaling things, as if the explicit description of when I first went to bed with my husband's friend were an offense against propriety. Honestly, I'm fed up with all this watching your P's and Q's, kowtowing to the propriety and bourgeois morality I was brought up on, worried sick about how this or that will look, the mother's proper role in the family, the daughters' virginity. As if mothers and daughters didn't have a sex and didn't just legitimately heat up at the sight of a healthy normal male. Well, let me tell you, me who my whole life tried to act and react as if I didn't have a sex, embarrassed and confused when I'd get a thrill out of erotic scenes in movies or books, here I was, the exemplary mother of a family, the obedient and self-effacing daughter, the chaste and virtuous wife, so timid and so pure, so innocent and so naive, me, now I'm proclaiming the legitimacy of the pleasure you go out and get just because that's what you want, with whoever you want it with, and marriage doesn't enter into it.

The woman who writes me has already started to shake her head and her finger, look at her now, a lowdown hussy, who experimented in all sorts of ways, just to prove that there weren't any limits on her freedom. Look at her, now she wants to give me a lesson in morality. No, now I don't want her to speak. She'll have to cool her heels. She can keep her peace right here in these pages, just stick to writing me. It was because of her kicking over the traces that I pulled back and got scared, missed out on the best years of my youth, fed on my guilt complexes.

For the first time in my life, I've come to feel freely, wholly, fully female. And eager. This sensation gives me a dizzy rush, a joy I never felt before or even suspected. I don't want to be tied to anybody. The bonds of love are just another form of captivity. All I want and hope for is to live the moment. It's enough. And later? Later I'll think about it, look into it. All I care about is now. Female. And eager. My meetings with my husband's friend took place in my apartment. Every day. Getting naked is teaching me mysteries my body knew nothing about. I never supposed my skin held so many violent and delicate sensations. The dark recesses of my depths open up rare, new dimensions every day. In learning to know my lands and my seas, I'm beginning to feel a strong drive to leave these walls behind, get out on the streets, discover places I've never been.

My friend is afraid to be seen with me. His problem is his family, his wife, his children. Not to mention being my husband's friend. All his qualms, this sneaking around. I'm not interested in any of that. I don't want to go on being stuck in the apartment. Before long I'll have a lot of men friends. I know who I can call up to get started on my plan. To hang out in places I've never been, where artists and intellectuals go, where maybe somebody will take an interest in my writing, stashed away for so many years.

I open the window. The pungent smell of ripe fruit doesn't make me take any deep breaths, my eyes shut. The wind from off the sea swoops around my freshly bathed body, but without sending an electric shiver of pleasure through me. He'll come tonight. Just as he's come every night. Are you home alone? All his qualms, this sneaking around. I wear filmy layers on my skin, on my body, to be slowly peeled away right down to the bare skin. My friend has soft delicate hands, not sweaty, but my body already knows his soft delicate hands, which no longer dream up anything new. I want to get away from the four walls of my apartment.

I know I want to set out in search of new experiences. Female and eager. No, definitely, I'm not happy with my friend's excessive caution, scared to take me out, because somebody might spot him. All his qualms, this sneaking around. I must let the woman who writes me speak.

You've nothing left to lose. Your family fell apart, while his to some extent continues to hold together. He and his wife get along reasonably well, manage to bring up their children also reasonably well. It's not fair to bring all this crashing down, just because of your ridiculous thirst for new experiences. Ridiculous thirst, yes, indeed, you're acting like a teenager and, at your age, to act that way has gotten comical and ludicrous.

Comical and ludicrous indeed. The woman who writes me likes to ridicule me. Every time I made a fool of myself and other people laughed, she was always right there, egging them on. Honestly, I do feel like a teenager, I didn't live through those years. In my adolescence, flutterings and mutilated desires. More than fair, before old age sets in, for me to hurry up and live a little, I've missed so much already. I got tired of facing the end, sour, tied in knots, with no one around, except for the dismal company of the woman who writes me. You think it's ridiculous that I, at forty-five, make that forty-six, a year has already passed since this story began, you think it's ridiculous for me at my age to feel female? And eager? And desire a man? When here I never got the least pleasure out of life? You think it's ridiculous for me to act like a victim now? Well fine, you just go think what you want, go ahead and laugh, laugh your head off, I know my mirrors don't deceive me. The man who's been coming to make love to me these nights wouldn't come if I couldn't make him feel he wanted me. He's anxious to come here, are you all alone? eager hands, soft delicate hands, not sweaty, me giving in, mouth on mouth, he thinks I'm pretty making love, thinks I'm beautiful, my filmy clothes, provocative, sensual, peeled away slowly down to the bare skin, him making love to me, thinking I'm beautiful.

And you believe it. Don't you realize that filmy negligees don't go with anything but a young body, a young face? It's no accident you turn down the lights, pretending it's more romantic with the lights down low, which, you have to admit, covers up your wrinkles, the curves you haven't got. The man can't get pleasure out of being with you, if you're artificial, working at being sexy in a way that's not spontaneous because it's forced. Quite a while back, your husband tried to have an affair with his wife and now he's having fun getting even, making a big thing of this affair with you. Don't think your friend is impressed with your last-gasp sensuality. He has an interest in keeping his family together and has already seen how much he had to lose in these encounters. No use trying to draw him in because, besides not loving you, he's tired of your ridiculous thirst for new experiences. Despite everything, you know your conscience would hurt terribly if you broke up a home.

I'm impressed to hear such talk from a person who never gave this sort of thing a second thought, when it was something she wanted. She pretends she's forgotten her father died because of her. At a time when young women didn't live by themselves, she left home to live free and easy, far from the reproofs of her father, who didn't care for her rebel ways. He had a heart condition, the blow was too much for him. Right away, his heart attack, right after that, his death. She never felt remorse, it never even upset her. She had the nerve to say her father blackmailed her to the nth degree. He probably wanted his heart attack to make her feel guilty. That's why the woman who writes me didn't accept any guilt. She pretends she's forgotten the unhappy ending to the marriage of over thirty years which she broke up because the old guy believed she really loved him—the femme fatale. She merely wanted to find out how far she could get on sheer physical attraction. Flighty, petty, irresponsible, and inconsistent, she didn't realize how full of harm she was.

To this day you confuse the need to be independent with stories of running away from home and making someone die from the shock of it. A father who's very ill is one who can die at any moment. What you consider playing around was no more than youthful high spirits and not what broke up a marriage already on the rocks. No one was to blame. No one. No, no, no.

The woman who writes me is desperate because she can't say I. She has no way to make excuses for herself, no way to defend herself. When you make excuses, there's something that needs excusing. Self-defense is self-condemnation. And when you start justifying and defending yourself, it brings out guilt and condemnation. She has no I. She's the other. I am I. I condemned myself, I accused myself, I blamed myself, I lived through my failure, little by little, until it wore me out. That's why every last inch of me is free. She never broke free. She'll never break free. And she'll always be tied down, because she can't confront her own guilt head on. She can only get in a glancing blow. Off center, at cross-purposes with herself, she has no knowledge of her I. Done in by a single letter. In one letter I am I. And in my faces in the mirror. I?

The hot night outside. The doorbell. Are you alone? Oh, what silly foolish fears. Yes. No. Yes. No. I don't want to stay shut up at home. Either we go out to dinner or it's all over between us. Everything's over? Your qualms, your sneaking around. I'm fed up. That's it. Yes. No. Yes. No. Finally. The hot night outside. The seashore. The view is nicer from here. I want to sit in front of the window. Over by the palm tree. Good evening, what will you have to drink? Have you decided what you'll have for dinner? But what silly foolish fears. Yes, no. I don't want to stay home any more, is that clear? Either we go out every night, or it's all over between us. All over? The hot night. The doorbell. Are you alone? Where'll we go today? Where tomorrow? Why bother being discreet? Here you are getting all edgy again, always scared, how boring. You silly ass. Yes. No. Yes. Do you like my dress? Why be more discreet? You're the one who's afraid of everybody, not me, I'm free, I am. Yes. No. I want you to introduce me to that painter friend of yours. I want you to introduce me to that poet friend of yours. No. Yes. I'll call anybody I want to. They're my friends. Today we're going to that lecture. Today we're going to the movies. Today we're going over to see . . . Today we're going to that seaside restaurant. Yes. No. Why? Today we're going to that book-signing party for . . . Today we're going to play cards at . . . I'll drink as much as I want to. Yes. No. Your wife. She's been crying a lot? It's only natural, she wasn't prepared psychologically, she'll get used to it. You'll have to leave your wife. Either me or her. No. Yes. No. Or it's all over between us. Either me or her, nothing less. It's all over? Why can't it be done in a hurry? Well, I'm telling you it's got to be done in a hurry. We don't have much time, we've got to make the most of it, we've already lost a lot, where'll we go today? How nice, I'm not drunk, no, yes, my dress is not indecent, you're the one with the dirty mind, where'll we go today? I want to go to that art show by . . . if you don't want to come with me, it's all right, I'll go there by myself, I'll meet up with . . . I'll go if I want to, I'll do what I want to do. Did I go out this afternoon? But I told you I was going out. I told you I was going to see . . . I told him I'd show him my stories. He's your friend, you were the one who introduced me to him, don't be silly. You want to know something? I'm talking too much, I don't owe you an apology. I like this record. Come over here. The window's open. The wind, is that mango? What scent is that, not getting through my pores? I'm cold, I want to keep my blouse buttoned up, very cold, no, I just want to listen to music, no, I'm cold, please don't insist, no, yes, you don't care if he liked my stories? He was amazed to see how I could write those things, think up those incidents, tied down there at home, not sharing ideas or having any contact with writers, just reading whatever came to me. Oh, no, please, don't go telling me you're a tiny bit jealous now, oh, no, you're really silly. Yes. No. My stories. He thought my stories had a lot of power. Yes, I'm only talking about my stories. If you don't like it, too bad, you know where the door is. You'll be back tomorrow? If you don't want to, you don't need to come back ever again. So. The open window. The hot night outside. The doorbell. I'm all alone, yes, silly boy. No, today we're not going anywhere. I'm tired, I don't want to go out. Very tired. I don't know why. I just don't feel like going out. Let's call . . . They can come over here, we can chat, we can have a drink, don't worry, silly, I'm not going to drink too much, I'll be very nice, a good little girl, well behaved so daddy won't scold, okay? Put on a little music. Put in an ice cube. Want to turn the volume down? No? Because I like it up loud. But that way we can't talk to each other. But that way the neighbors will complain. But this isn't any wild kid party. Well, let's just go wild and see if any neighbor has the courage to come over here and complain. You love to kid around. I'm not kidding. Great, the people I invited are all here, you know everybody, who brought the guitar? wonderful, turn off the sound, live is better, everybody make themselves at home, everybody do whatever they feel like, if there isn't room for me, no problem, I'll sit on somebody's lap, I'll do what I want to, silly boy, anybody who wants to think it's wrong can think so, I don't mind, who'll find me a nice little lap? not you, I need a nice soft little lap, anybody who wants whiskey just get it off the table, beer is in the refrigerator, everybody look after themselves, don't be silly, I'm not drunk, I'm not, but I'm going to be, right? Don't be silly, how in the world can you call this a wild party? If the neighbors are bothered, let them move, to hell with them, yes, no, yes, and to hell with you too, you worry too much about other people, what other people must be thinking, what other people must be saying, yackety-yack, I've had enough, I've told you a thousand times I don't owe anybody any apologies for my life, those days are over, today I'm completely free, if you're not, that's your problem, you should've learned to be by now, all right, it's not all right. All right. The wind from off the sea. The sacred mango tree with its solitary fruit. The hot night outside. Night blotted out in its foliage. All right, where are we going tonight? You're silly. I am being discreet. I can't just stand here and say nothing. I'm not going to stop talking to people, you're being disagreeable. If you're in a better humor, come back tomorrow, if not, don't come back tomorrow or any time. The solitude of the fruit on the sacred mango. The open window. The wind from off the sea. The doorbell. The doorbell? No, I'm not alone. You know him, it's your friend, silly. What's wrong with that, he only came to talk about my stories. Not so loud. Don't give it a thought, darling, he just gets like that, he's a silly ass, he started getting jealous of me, it's better for him to be on his way than to stay here getting on everybody's nerves, now don't tell me, he's holding the elevator, waiting for me to go get him, but I won't, he's got to learn not to be possessive, right, darling? will you have another whiskey? The open window. The wind from off the sea. Do you want me to read, darling? All right I'll read. I found my face in the corner of the final mirror. I want to keep this new smile just the way it is, right where that tear trickled down. Lapses. Fruit tree blossoming in the deepest of shadows. Why do you want me to read them, you already read them, my dear. You like my voice, the silences of my voice. How nice you enjoyed my stories. Publish them? It's up to you, darling. I want another ice cube. The open window. The wind from off the sea. The scent of ripe fruit. The wind from off the sea penetrating my pores through my half-open blouse. My open blouse. The ripe pulp of the fruit. The fur rug. Don't turn on the other light. The wind from off the sea. The ocean wave. Silent and warm. Night wave in the night of my depths. Rhythmic breathing in my transfigured night. Darling. I want to keep this new smile just the way it is, right where that tear trickled down. Lapses. Fruit tree blossoming. The open window. The closed window. The solitude of my pores. The doorbell. Are you alone? Are you drunk? Go away, I don't want to see you ever again. But are you alone? Oh, not again, yes, I'm alone. And I'm alone because I want to be. At times, you need to stop, to take time out to think and feel, nobody breathing down your neck. At times, I feel confused. Do you want to help me? Well, silly, I need you, who told you I didn't? You silly, silly boy. Where'll we go today? Let's go to the restaurant and that table over by the coconut palm, remember? Just the two of us. The deep curve of the shoreline. The wind from off the sea, comes from the sea right up by my face. I let the wind blow through my hair. A man and a woman right beside the rustling of the ancient mango tree. Soft delicate hands caressing my skin on the fur rug. I like you, silly, you sweet silly man. The good smell of ripe fruit. The hot night outside. The solitary fruit up among the rustling leaves. The window wide open. Solitude. The doorbell. Are you alone? Tonight we're going to do the clubs. No, I don't want to stay at home. I want to see people, lots of people. No. Yes. No. Either you stop this nonsense, or it's all over between us. Over? Yes. No. Silly boy. Hi, everybody. Hi. Hi. Why bother being more discreet? I'm not making things difficult for you, yeah, yeah, I've heard all this before. Stop it. No. Yes. The doorbell. The doorbell? Are you alone? No, you know each other, you're the one who introduced me to him, he came to ask me to his art show. You're on your way? You can go. Never mind him, my darling, he had a prior engagement he'd forgotten. No, I've never posed. I don't think I'd have the patience to pose. My profile. With my hair loose. The wind from off the sea blowing through my hair. No, I won't pose, darling, not here or anywhere else. You'll illustrate my poems? The wind, ah, the wind from off the sea. The fruit snuggling on the branches. The smell of ripe fruit. Expert, experienced hands. The ocean wave. Night wave in the nights of my confusion. The labored breathing in my transfigured night. Darling. No, I won't pose. The open window. The hot night outside. The solitude pressing in. The doorbell. No, I'm not making things hard for you, you don't try to understand things, you're silly. Where are we going tonight? I want to go do the clubs. I'm not tired of clubs because this one is new. No, I'm not making things hard for you. Let's go dancing. Why bother being more discreet? No. Yes. Your wife? She's here? Who's she with? Wonderful, fantastic, unbelievable. With my husband. You're jealous of my husband? My husband is jealous of me? Your wife is jealous of you? Well, I'm not jealous of anybody. Let's dance, that's it, hold me tight, very tight, I want us just glued together, that's it, face against face, sex on sex, don't be silly, you silly boy, hold me, don't let me go, no, yes, no. Marvelous, is he looking? Is she looking, great, I don't want to get even, I just want them to see, don't be silly, you don't owe anybody any apologies, your life's your own, you don't have to demand any apologies, hi, my dear, all right, we'll talk about getting the book out, darling, you said you'd come back? I don't even remember, all right, later we'll sit down and discuss it, now I have to go back to that silly man's table, all right, I'll expect you tomorrow for sure, darling. Why bother being more discreet? No. Yes. No. No, I'm not drunk. I'm feeling very good. This night is beyond all. This night is solitude. The closed window. The hot night outside. The open window. No, I can't feel the wind from off the sea. I can't smell ripe fruit. I'm alone. Yes I'm alone, silly. Not again. Yes. No. Yes. No. No. Oh, no. Just no. No. Stop thinking you broke up your home on account of me. Stop saying I hurt you. If you'd been getting along with your wife, as you keep telling me you had, you wouldn't have come here to see me with that song and dance about life insurance. I'm tired of hearing you say over and over how I broke up your home, oh, yes, a fine home, a fine pile of shit. No. Yes. Well I'm going to tell you something I hadn't meant to tell, just out of sheer consideration. Consideration, no, commiseration, compassion, pity. Lots of pity. You really want to know? You think you can take it? Your oh so virtuous wife, so chaste, so pure, that wife you think would have to be in total shock before she'd take up with the likes of my husband, poor woman, so mixed up, and you're feeling responsible for leaving her and seeing her run around now with all sorts of men, well, just listen, silly ass, your oh so virtuous wife, so chaste, so pure, so sluttish, your slut of a wife, slut, right? For years your slut of a wife has been having an affair, you want to know who with? Can't you guess? Then guess, silly, stupid, an affair with my husband, mine. You don't believe me? Great, you're even more stupid than I thought. One of your children looks a lot like you, isn't that right, you big macho? Did you ever notice who the other one looks like? Stupid, it's as plain as the nose on your face. No. Yes. NO. YES. NOOOO. YESSSS. I open the window. The silence of the fruit on the branches. The hot night out beyond the mango tree and the wind. The ancient mango tree. The wind from off the sea. I close the window. The doorbell? Nobody. Solitude invades the most secret of my pores. No smells waft into the air. Silence. Deep silence beyond the branches. Silence in my eyelids. My skin is quiet. The closed window. The telephone. What? Is he ever dumb. Are you sure? But I was only joking. I wanted to get rid of him, that's all. In this day and age, to try to kill his wife, just because somebody said that she was cheating on him? Impossible. You'd have to be an absolute idiot. She's in the hospital? I sure hope the police don't come around taking up my time. Do you really suppose he didn't mention my name? Worse? There's more bad news? Oh, don't tell me that. Her son? He tried to kill the son? That too? Great, now we have all the makings of tragedy. Attempted suicide. The whole family in the hospital. But after all, did anybody actually die from any of this madness? Right you are. Right. Right. Yes, darling. I'm not doing anything tonight. Getting my book of stories out. Okay. I'll expect you. Come on over, darling.

23

Strange indeed the attitude of the woman who writes me. All of a sudden she doesn't even try to get back at me. And if I tell you this, you're probably not going to believe me. She's crying. She thinks she's to blame for what she calls my present cynicism. Do you all think I'm cynical? Honestly, I can't feel things the way I used to. At times, it seems to me I can't feel anything at all. Just sensations. Not happiness not sadness. Not sorrow not anguish. Not disgust not regret. As if I'd already felt everything there was to feel. It's all over. No. I can still feel irritation. I feel fatigue. I feel boredom. Nothing more.

I open the window. The ancient mango tree is weighted down. Weighted down with fruit. Green? Ripe? Rotting fruit. The ancient mango tree weighted down with rotting fruit. The wind from off the sea brings the smell of rotting fruit. The birds have left the nests that snuggled in the curve of the branches. The abandoned nests. But their young.

I close the window.

I close my eyes.

I close my hands.

I close the door to my mirrors.

24

The mirrors. But with lights off. Images shut out, images going nowhere. Caught outside the mirror, I want to get back in and I can't. Hazy glimmers seep through the cracks and outline a hazy figure. Who is the shadow roaming the mirrors? The faceless, expressionless shadow. My spent hands slide along the glass wall. It's very cold. I'm very cold. It's impenetrable. I'm impenetrable. The thick shadows from hazy stragglers of light. Walled-off things and bodies that touch, clash, wear out. Converge to diverge. Circle in the darkened mirrors. Hazy thick shadows, where's the face? The faces? I don't want to see my face. My face, no face. No, I can't see my feet. What ground am I not standing on? I don't inhabit my body's space.

The doorbell. I don't move. Insistently the irritating ring. I go up to the door. I don't open it. Are you alone? I'm not home.

The woman who writes me has feet gnawed at by rats. When she was little, as punishment, her father used to leave her locked up in the attic at home. But punishment had no effect on her and she kept right on, no matter how much he threatened her. She didn't seem to be afraid of anything. She laughed at the rats that at night would come to gnaw at my feet. Laughing at my fears. Fear of the rats. Fear of punishment. Fear of disobeying. Her laughter. What'll happen if we do disobey? The woman who writes me used to laugh and laugh. But the rats aren't the trained kind. What do you mean, there aren't any rats? What about the noise they made? What about my feet they gnawed at? And the smell? And the stench?

The woman who writes me has feet that are gnawed at by rats. She looks at her gnawed-at feet and falls down. I think this is very funny because I don't believe in rats. They don't exist. Rats are just a psychological mechanism. There have never been any rats. I live in a new building, on Seventh of September Avenue. Seventh floor. Clean stairways. Clean floors. Clean roots. Of the sacred mango tree. What are rats? Rats are all in the mind. Figments of the imagination. There's no such thing in cold hard fact. Rats are as unreal as werewolves and headless horsemen. Mental processes. The head gnaws at the feet of the woman who writes me. With tiny sharp relentless teeth. Rat teeth. Rat tongue. Rat feet. Tiny rat eyes. It's funny. Tiny magic animals, making little sounds that don't exist. Actually gnawing at made-up feet. Filling the woman who actually writes me with make-believe fear. The woman who writes me has now started believing in fantasies. Ghosts and sorcery. She believes in make-believe. She looks at her feet and the truth of them knocks her down. I laugh. Laugh and laugh. The breath of the woman who writes me smells like rats. I open the window and let in the wind from off the sea. The woman who writes me goes up in the attic and locks herself up in her memories. Her thin cries, her shrill whining, her feeble rat squeak irritate me. I open the window wider. The rats can't eat the mangoes dangling from the sagging limbs. The make-believe rats. The make-believe woman. Make-believe me. The wind of imagination comes from the sea of truth. I smell the smell of ripe mangoes. I actually smell the imaginary mangoes. The actual mango tree in the age of make-believe. The imaginary authoress, lost amid made-up truths. The made-up things I say are truths. The truths I say are make-believe. How much is there to make-believe? How could there be anything so made up there was no truth to it? Who's the truer? Me? The woman who writes me? The authoress? Do we exist or do we have any being?

I open the window.

I open my eyes.

I open my hands.

I open the doors to my mirrors.

26

A seed of hope. Promise. Yes, something is promised in the scent of ripe fruit the wind brings. The wind from off the sea. Water washing my body. The bubbling soapsuds bursting in the cold spray of the shower. The liquid motion of my rippling skin. My skin, so washed, so clean. So fragrant. My skin, so soft. So eager. My skin, so smooth.

Your wrinkled skin. Your skin, so rough.

My skin glides under the touch of dry delicate hands. The dry delicate hands of a man who believes in me. In my talent. In the power of my perceptions. He admires me. He desires me. For the purity of my characters. For the softness of my skin.

He's very curious about you. He's a successful writer, who likes to live out the experiences of his characters. He's concerned with observing the reactions of a neurotic woman in the pre-senile phase. You offer excellent material for someone wanting to analyze this question.

The doorbell. My half-open blouse. I go to the door almost smiling. Meaningful looks. Whiskey? Ice? The delicate dry hands. Him calling me soft. Me feeling smooth. Skin gliding across skin. The wind from off the sea. The scent of ripe fruit. The faint wave on the dark beach. Eager? Female? Insatiable? Sexy? What? I don't scratch, I chew my fingernails. The faint wave on the dark beach. My body against the fur rug. The wind from off the sea, wafting over my open body. No, I don't care to smoke. No, I don't care to drink. No, no, not over there, those are my mirrors, don't open them, please. Come look at the sacred mango tree. In the distance, the beat of ritual drums crisscrossing the warm night. Close by, the beat of the beating in the wind from off the sea. Off the sea that comes from afar. Now a surprise. What surprise? The dry delicate hands holding a fat briefcase. The manuscript of your latest novel? Okay, I'll open it. The title page? The dedication? You dedicated your novel to me? What? Now I'm your character? A character in your next novel? You too are this moment happening, in my pages. Who? Where?

Now I want to be alone. My body liquid under the water's skin. The artificial scent of soap, mixed with the natural smell of mango. My watery skin. I put on my robe. I go to the window. Night crisscrossed in the beat of ritual drums, coming nearer and nearer. Tomorrow I'll go to the book-signing party for . . . Before long I'll be premiering my own book. My first book. I'll run into the same old crowd at the autographing party for . . . When I premiere my book, the same old crowd will be there too. Tomorrow, perhaps I won't feel like chatting. I step back a bit, look at people and ask myself, are they made up or real? If they're make-believe, isn't it more than likely they're for real? Are they like me? If I start telling here what these people are saying, they'll start belonging to me as characters of mine. Where are they? In my words? Or in their words? There comes my novelist friend. There comes my publisher friend. They're imaginary. He comes up to me. Who? He looks at me. His knowing look. His smoldering eyes. Come on. It's stifling in here. I open the window. Slender, hurried hands. The wind from off the sea blows through the attic windows of my pores. The distant wave spills out over the beach. His smoldering eyes. His slender, hurried hands. A quick wave. A beach that isn't a beach. I want to be alone. I breathe in deep the scent of ripe mango. I can touch my solitude. I think of the dry, delicate hands caressing my soft skin.

You can't go on leading this disorderly life, first with one man, then with another. You seem to have forgotten the poor fellow who almost killed his wife and his son because of you. You need to get your life in order. You need to think about your sons. They need you more than ever. They're ashamed of your irresponsible behavior as a lewd, licentious woman, an unprincipled hussy who turns sex not into something pleasurable, but into a way of making a statement, to prove to yourself you can attract every last man that comes along. You want to scandalize and shock people with a degenerate way of life that can only bring disaster down on you and your sons.

The woman who writes me is envious of me. She's envious of the men who admire me. She's envious of my literary work. She can't bear the thought that I've signed a contract with a big publishing house. She always traveled in intellectual and artistic circles, but she never managed to write anything serious. You want to know why? Because she didn't live life seriously. She was always frivolous. I lived out in all seriousness the worst lies of my disillusionment. I erred in all seriousness. I erred responsibly. She was frivolously right. When she was right. It's the worst kind of error. When her father died, she refused to go to the cemetery, because she detested formalities. Now, she wants to go every day. What for? She takes flowers, with a cloying display of remorse. No, I don't hate her. She resembles me superficially in my list of disillusionments. Just the shell. Deep down, she's nothing like me.

Something is promised in the scent of ripe fruit that the wind brings. The doorbell? Nobody. In my stark solitude, I think of the dry, delicate hands caressing my soft skin.

You're the man who in the next few minutes is going to have to get busy and give me the biggest orgasm any woman can ever hope for or imagine. Your slender, dry hands, gliding over my soft skin. I'll appear in your novel as the sex-starved woman, searching for the heights of pleasure. Voracious. Insatiable. The excitement of unplumbed depths. The urge to let out an impossible scream. You'll invade my own novel, for a brief moment, a male who doesn't need to be macho, though you think you have just the sex needed to reach clear inside me and bring out the perfect scream of fusion. You won't be that good. Despite the wind from off the sea. Despite your slender, dry hands, gliding over my soft skin. Despite the warm scent of ripe fruit. You won't be that good. Despite the sea surge. Your plunge is an opening, but only brings a sigh, that can never grow into a full-throated scream. But you're good and firm and whole and my skin glides softly under yours. I feel almost compelled to give in to your inventions, since you see me as taking my full of sexual pleasure. In the meantime, my dear friend, I'm condemned by what I've invented for myself, the unremitting, forever fruitless search. You won't give me what I desire. No one will. No one? Ah, if the wheel of life, turning and returning, comes round at just the right moment, stops at the right spot, then I'll know. The sudden turn, the discovery. But only if life rotates, with a precision that knows no before or after, a moment unique in time. No, you won't give me what I desire. In your novel, I won't be me any longer. The ring you gave me is an impossible invention. I don't wear rings. The only ring I used to wear was my wedding band. Once the marriage was over, the ring was too. There's nothing binding me to the world. Yes, tonight, just for tonight, I'll wear your ring. Tonight is ours, but don't tell me you love me. You're just interested in me. No, don't call me doll. That's so old. It's silly. I'm thinking about my doll. The prettiest doll I ever had. Its china face broken all to smithereens. Can you see on top of the bookcase? A patchwork raggedy doll. Ugly, but pretty. When I was little, my nanna used to make dolls for me out of scraps. I've never come across such sad dolls again. This one came from Paraíba. Sad-happy. I like her. Pretty in an ugly kind of way. Is someone ringing the doorbell?

Someone is trying to get in. Is it you, son? Who's with me? He's a friend. A novelist. But I don't owe you any explanations about my life. You or anybody else. You're drunk. You've no right to be interrogating me. And here you're trying to tell me you're not drunk. You can barely stand up. But what is it you want, son? You never came back home again. What happened? If you mean to stay home, then go to your room. I told you he's a friend. I have anyone over I please. You have a dirty mind, like your father. What do you mean? Take your hands off your mother. And don't you go telling me what you think of my friends. Don't give me that look. You're all upset, that's it. Upset and drunk. Yes, drunk. You shouldn't drink so much. Go to your room. And watch out you don't fall down. Go to your room, I'll bring you some coffee. Don't you talk that way about your mother, getting old, being a whore. You've no business doing that. I won't allow it. Shut up, you're talking nonsense. You've got to stop drinking and watch what you're saying about your mother. I have absolute authority, you hear me, I have absolute authority to tell you the truth. To tell you you're a big mess. I got tired of defending you, you and your brothers. I sacrificed myself. I walked through fire. I turned to ashes. Now I've had enough. I, your own mother, will do what I want to and I won't have any son of mine coming in here and telling me what's right and what's wrong. Go to your room, I repeat. You've no reason to go through the living room. I can have anybody I want over. And if I go out with a lot of men, it's my problem. You have no business interfering. What's going on here, boy? Who gave you that gun? Go to your room, I told you. Son, don't do anything foolish. No. Please give me the gun. Sweetheart, mommy is begging you. Come here, my darling. He's someone I've known. He's arranging a book-signing party for one of mommy's books. That's all. Come here, I'll introduce you to him, you'll see. Now don't be angry, sweetheart. Give me the gun. That's a good boy. Be calm. You're all upset. There's no reason to be, sweetie baby. Sit down here. I'll bring you some coffee. Why don't you take a bath? Don't go away, sweetie. Sleep here. Why not?

What a scare that boy gave me. He almost did something foolish. Fortunately you handled it right. Thanks. Please go now. It's not our night. He may come back. And in the state he's in, no telling what he might do. I never could be firm with my sons. I'd even forgotten about their problems. I gave up the struggle because my sacrifice wasn't doing any good. I don't want to think about it any more. When there's no solution, it's useless to keep on. Their father doesn't do anything. How can I face up to a hopeless situation by myself, I want to forget. There's nothing anyone can do. I've decided to put these problems out of my mind. Please go. I want to be by myself. Take your ring. All right, all right. I'll keep the ring. But, please, go now. I want to be alone.

Alone. In the solidarity of my solitude. I want water. Water splashing off my head, my back, all over me. Water frees me from all those scales and crusts. My skin made of water. My light body, my washed body, my clean body. I go to the window. I breathe the wind from off the sea. I take the ring off my finger and throw it, far away, into the heart of night growing among the leaves of the sacred mango tree. Am I free?

28

Yesterday I walked through the Terreiro de Jesus Square and sat down at one of the little tables in front of the Cantina da Lua, at the corner of Portas do Carmo Street. Sitting there, I could watch four hundred years of Bahia history passing by. Were black people shinier before slavery was abolished? The sugarcane vendor, with his basket of stalks, has been there for four hundred years, the same white teeth against the darkness of his face. These shapely mulatto women and the stouter black ones are the same ones that excited Gregório de Matos, whose house is a bit farther on. This bare-chested black man, really good-looking, sitting there on a box, beneath the wide brim of his straw hat, his beard and hair flecked with white, an African buffalo horn necklace, his curved pipe silent, how old could he be? How many centuries old? This little brown-skinned prostitute, pausing in front of the table across, can't possibly be eighteen. The blond fellow who sells handcrafts in the Plaza, comes over and asks for a Brahma beer. The little brown-skinned prostitute gives the blond man a hug and says she's pregnant. No one's surprised. No one cries. No one laughs. They pass by. The same as it ever was. For four hundred years they've been passing by. The twanging of the *berimbau*, to the rhythm of the stylized *capoeira*, the pungent sweat of the fighter-dancers. Then, suddenly the magician, with bright flowing robes and top hat. A minstrel? The ice cream man hawks *mangaba* flavor, on top of his head a cooler that looks like a pail? Like a tub? The police make their rounds. I order another rum *batida*. I look and don't look. I'm alone and with everyone. I buy a small package of fried peanuts and ask a child where is his mother? She's working. Where? In the red-light district. I run my hand over the head of the little son of a whore, what are you going to be when you grow up? With a feminine little flick of his wrist, he answers he's going to be a doctor. He wanted to buy his mother a big house, a cabaret. In the large building where the School of Medicine used to be, they've installed the Center for Bahian Studies and the Center for Afro-Oriental Studies. Under their windows, the incense fumes. The piercing smell washing in stronger still, carried on the wave of the wind. Always rising, the perfumed smoke of live coals in the clay incense burner. Old people and young around the little tables. Talking. Sitting in silence. Drinking. Smoking. Marijuana? Blacks and mulattoes and whites and browns and blonds. The ancient is new. The new is very old. The mulatto girl, forever young, goes past the *umbu* fruit stand. Yesterday and today and always, the vendor runs his hand over her well-made butt, she's smiling, picking an *umbu* off the tray, going on her way, looking back, taking a bite out of the yellowish green of the fruit. Real and invented characters, in a true and fantastic time, in the unreal space of an old-new square, surrounded by the townhouses of many yesterdays ago, plus its three churches and two in the distance. From my little table, I can read the sign "Cantina da Lua," with some stars around it. Why the name "Cantina of the Moon"? I pay my bill, get up, and keep on to the left, averting my eyes from the funeral parlor, I go down Maciel Street. I go slowly, looking over and over again at the whores, the mothers of the whores, the daughters of the whores, all waiting for work, sitting in the doorways, grubby clothes, their eyes eying me and me feeling a strange shame, as if I had been caught going through other peoples' things, things not my own. What business do I have being here? From a seedy bar comes the blare of a radio. I stop. I look in. Three couples dancing. Hard to say who are the shabbiest? The women barefoot, with dirty feet, chipped color on their nails, faded clothing on worn-out skin. The men in old tennis shoes, one of them in Hawaiian thongs, the other barefoot. Who are the shabbiest? A cockroach skittering between their feet. They kept right on dancing. The couples very close, sex against sex. Sexes consumed by disease and filth. They went on dancing, rubbing up against each other, the radio blaring, in that maddeningly sunny afternoon. In front of me, the dancers, their diseased sexes too close, too fused to be thinking about catching anything. I kept watching. They watched me. They smiled, lasciviously. Little by little, they stopped smiling. They stopped watching me. Slowing their rhythm. Stopping the sexual contact. The radio blaring. And me still watching. They stopped watching me. They went and sat down in a corner of the bar. Heads down, looking tired. Sitting down, wordless, in front of their empty glasses. Empty. Emptied. Who am I, standing here, on a seamy street in the red-light district, in the middle of a stunningly sunny mid-afternoon, a radio blaring out rock music? Who am I, that I don't have the courage to go in the stinking bar and order those empty glasses to be filled? Who am I, eyes to the ground, ashamed of myself? What business did I have barging in there, all curiosity, special and safe, just taking in the local color? I keep on my way, always on down toward the Whipping Post. Seeing nothing else at all, unless it's the jagged and smooth rocks under my slow feet.

29

The woman who writes me, once again, doesn't want to put me on paper any more. However, I know how to get her to the typewriter. After all those months of seclusion in the attic of her former house, she can't stand being alone any more. She can hardly walk, her feet gnawed at, soiled by rats. The rats I deny and exist only in her mind. And in her feet, of course. The guilt of her rats. The rats of her guilt.

The woman who writes me has, just lately, been thinking of marriage. Just imagine. The old pussycat. She wanted to meet a man who'd love her. She wanted a home and a family, the kind of family setup everybody is familiar with. That's a lot to hope for. The men she's acquainted with knew about her uninhibited sex life, which she accepted and defended. She wants to get married.

The woman who writes me has to go on writing me. Come what may. I know what I'll do. I won't make fun of that old flame. The biology teacher. Never without a coat and tie. His degree now in hand, a teacher of hers. There she was, unfastening her blouse and bra, leaning across the table, where he was trying to open his grade book to call the roll. The way she laughed at his red face. And him, wanting to look, but not looking. For two years she's been egging him on. One day, she went to his house, to borrow a book for an exam. She threw herself into his arms, his face very red, coat and tie, glasses falling off, no, don't do that. She didn't. She went away laughing. He has always kept up with her from a distance, Christmas card, birthday, a lot of laughs from her, more red faces whenever he was near her. The years went by, man after man came into her life, but no woman into his. Coat and tie, biology teacher, in the same high school.

To keep on putting me on paper, the woman who writes me has to keep on living. And to keep living, she needs somebody for company, in her despair and her repentance and her remorse. She needs somebody to help her bear her own guilt. Someone to free her from the rats. Who? Him. The biology teacher. Dangling there in his glasses, coat and tie, always turning red whenever he came near her.

They met offhandedly, casually, of course. He'd turn redder than ever. She didn't laugh. Her blouse buttoned all the way up, how are you, sir? Circumspect phone calls, ceremonious visits, *jenipapo* fruit liqueur at her house, homemade, if you please, her blouse buttoned clear to the neck, they decided to get married.

When he comes home after class, he takes off his coat and tie, puts on his striped pajamas. She's all solicitous, here are your slippers, do you want water or milk? She fixes dinner to suit him, not much seasoning, no fat, a dieter's meal, because of his ulcer. After dinner, they go watch television, sitting side by side on the living room sofa. Now and then she asks if he'd like a glass of milk. They're living in Brotas, in a little house off from the others, little white window curtains, cute crocheted covers on the blender, a tiny heart hanging on the front door, welcome, a fine lace doily for the bread basket, all of it made by her, really nice. The only thing lacking now is a baby, to make the couple's happiness complete. Wedded bliss.

This way she, the woman who writes me, will go on writing me. And will stop accusing me. At least for a while.

30

Do you want to go to Afro music night? Depends on who's going. My new friends are artists and intellectuals who love all kinds of popular culture, and almost all of them take an interest in the African roots of our culture.

Just lately I've started going to places where the common run of people gather, places people used to avoid in my father's and my husband's time as only fit for riffraff, blacks, drunks, scum, that is, people of no account. Young ladies of good family and self-respecting women have to know their place.

But where is my place? In the living rooms with crystal chandeliers, Sèvres statuettes, Portuguese silverware, Chinese porcelain vases, pure silk curtains, authentic colonial furniture, little tables with collections of antique pressing irons? Or as the night unfolds, inside the more powerful space, marked by the sound of drums and the metallic ring of agogôs?

I fit within many situations, I overflow in many directions. The light from off the crystal chandeliers fills my head with prisms, wraps my words in cellophane. Primitive rhythm slips off my ancient bonds, releases me from earlier prisons. Little by little, I've been untying a knot, loosening a noose, unmeshing a net, finally there's nothing to tie me down. My limitless liberated body rushes out in unimaginable rivers, hurtles over barriers I'd never even known were there.

Where is my place? The uncrossable is now, the impossible has happened. The wild dance comes down home to its roots, back to where it all began, grew pure again. The flow of time is compressed and condensed and then breaks free

109

and hurtles on, dares to say no to castrations and mutilations. I feel transparent and intact, in the clean lines of the swaying bodies, under the light fall of the all-pervading sound. For the first time, I feel it and live it to the core.

The black and mulatto bodies free to obey the sounds of ancestral drum beats, lose their shapes, melt into the rhythmic night. What a good-looking black man. What a good-looking black man up there on the platform. Long white pants flowing out wide, his bare chest crisscrossed with charm beads. The rhythm of his moves. His feet just barely touching down on the boards. What a good-looking black man. The ancient night. The primitive night.

From my father's house, I used to hear the beat from a *candomblé*, flooding out into the night, mingling into my sleep. The beat of the tall drums, sounding in the great black night. My nanna, her gaze lost in the distance, repeating, the drums of Xangô. Who is Xangô? Go to sleep, angel, go to sleep, you're not scared of lightning, not scared of thunder. My nanna's black hand, its nice warm roughness caressing my face. The medals throbbing under her starched white dress. My nanna, her gaze lost in the distance, I'd hold onto my nanna's black hand, go to sleep angel child. The heavy beat of the tall drums impregnating my sleep, flooding out into the night, the great black night. In those days, at my father's house, it was nasty to talk about, nasty to think about *candomblé*, something a white person should steer clear of. But Daddy, I'm not all that white, I'm dark. Hush up, girl.

What a good-looking black man. What a good-looking black man dancing up on the platform. What a good-looking little black boy. The black boy, son of the cook at the house next door. Walking on top of the wall that runs between the two yards. He sits down on top of the wall, his little head shaved bare, a medal strung on a cord around his neck. When it rains and it thunders, he runs for the yard, jumping and dancing and saying, his arms flung up in the air, he's king of the thunder, he's king of the lightning. My nanna crossing herself. In the afternoon sun, he's sitting on top of the wall. The wind from off the beach brings a whiff of the sea at low tide. He's sucking on a mango, smiling at me. The scent of the fruit, in the black boy's hand. Smiling. He holds a mango out to me. I scamper to my nanna's lap. What a good-looking little black boy. One day, he jumped over the wall. I was picking four-o'clocks over by the cistern. Made me jump. I turned around. He was pulling down his short pants, showing me, look here. Look here. His hard little sex. Look here. Once more he was dashing away to jump the wall. No one saw. Over by the cistern, my mind stayed on his hard little sex. What a good-looking little black boy. His grandmother was a slave. What about my great-great-grandparents? Where did I get my dark skin? From a whitening of the colors from Nigeria? From the hot winds breathed out of Guinea? What drums were beating when my blood first started flowing?

My limitless liberated body rushes out in unimaginable rivers, hurtles over barriers I'd never even known were there. The wild dance, coming down home to its roots, back to where it all began, growing pure again. I feel transparent and intact, in the clean lines of the swaying bodies, under the light fall of the all-pervading sound. What a good-looking black man up there on the platform. Long white pants flowing out wide, his bare chest crisscrossed with necklaces. The rhythm of his moves. His feet just barely touching down on the boards. Had his mother maybe been a cook in some house in Rio Vermelho? Had his grandmother been perhaps a slave on some plantation in the Recôncavo? Could he have been a descendant of the royal family? of some tribal chieftain? His blood flowing always true to the rhythm of the drums, free from the instruments found in drawing rooms hung with crystal chandeliers. What a good-looking black man. The flowing folds of his white pants moving with his body. The white pants cinched very tight at his waist. They don't fall with the fall of his body when he leaps. His firm, shiny muscles, standing out under the light bulbs. His smooth, lustrous skin, the outside of a fruit, night blooming.

Many times, no one would be looking, the black boy, son of the cook at the house next door, jumping over the wall, running over to the cistern, makes me jump, I turn around, he pulls down his short pants, look here, look here, running off again to jump the wall. Over by the cistern, I was thinking. The good-looking black man on the platform. The sound of the drums, the sound of the *agogô*. His smooth, shimmering body moving, moving in time. His flowing white pants cinched very tight at the waist. They don't fall with the fall of his body. I watch. Watching, following moves come down through generations.

Where is my place?

31

I like to take walks by myself, through these places where I used not to walk, or walked through in a hurry, eyes straight ahead. I used to look, but not really. Who looks when they look? Who knows what they know? These old townhouses in Pillory Square. No, I don't know. I look, wanting to look, wanting to find out. I don't understand these old townhouses, more time than space to them, in the layout of the Square. I'm standing in the middle of innumerable superimposed times joined by unknown emotions. Blurry. Thick. What're these tourists looking at, cameras in hand, wishing they could photograph the unphotographable? No way through the paint on these walls, the door frames, the windows. No safe way across the slipperiness of these rounded stones, smoothed by the passage of feet over time. There goes the little boy tugging his burro down the hill, saddlebags on each side heavy with fruit for market. Which of the alleys has real time in it? That ram tied in a doorway on Maciel Street, it isn't scared by the buses and taxis driving down the street. Those guinea hens scratching in front of the house, will they run out in the street? I walk along slowly, careful not to slip on the cobblestones, my feet unsure, not knowing where or when to step. Here is the Tempo, a restaurant with local fare. But Tempo is not time. The name of an Angolan deity. Tempo is more than time and its owner knows this. Its owner is the son of Time, smiling with his strands of shells and charm beads crisscrossed on his chest and around his body. He knows the future, guesses people's fate. Lord of many mysteries, I'm afraid to learn my fate. The power of his powerful seashells. I don't need to learn my fate, because I know my fate. I order a cup of sassafras tea. I sip idly, breathing in the scent of *dendê* palm oil, magical kitchen smells. I'm on my way, but I don't take leave of the man who reads life and knows death. The high priest of Time. I go up Portas do Carmo Street and come to the little tables in front of the Cantina da Lua bar. I see its sign dotted with stars. Sitting here, the oldest man and the likeliest to be found in the Terreiro de Jesus Square. Over his glass of beer, he smiles to me, the smile of still waters. Under the slow fluttering of the wide brim of his straw hat, thick layers of time overlaid on his black face, wrinkles without suffering or resentment. His limp jacket, colorful cotton tie against his knit shirt, the shirt of the Apaches of Tororó carnival group. A fisherman's hat protecting, guarding his face from the sun and the damp night air. Guarding the face of time. What about the strands of beads crisscrossing his tie? What are the colors of his god? He's smiling, the smile of still waters. The son of the goddess Janaína, who wants to take her son down to the bottom of the sea. Behind the brim of his straw hat with the wind gently fluttering it, the stars of the Cantina da Lua's sign. Today, smile of still waters, he's going to pray for me in the sanctuary. Can he really be lord of the mysteries, knower of the destinies of all people? Janaína's beads are blue and white. White and blue. And what if the bells started to ring, in the five churches, up above his huge fisherman's hat? Who is this black man, moves of a dancer, dressed all in white, coming into the Cantina da Lua? What a good-looking black man. Muscles bulging underneath his knit shirt. Such smooth skin. A chill runs through my body. He's the good-looking black man who was up on the platform, flowing white pants, bare chest crisscrossed with strands of beads, a dancer's walk. He walks among the little tables, moves of a dancer, and sits at the other end. I watch. He doesn't watch me. I look hard, wanting to see. Who is this good-looking black man, taking his seat without missing a beat? Who am I, chills through my body, wanting to look more than I'm looking? I want to go near him, but I don't budge. He doesn't look at me, no he doesn't look at me. I want to go over by him, but I don't go over by him. I'll go over. I won't go over. I'll go over. A shiver straight down to my sex, I've seen you dancing, you're a lovely dancer. He looks at me without looking at me, I look to get a better look. Up close, he's better looking. In the air, the strong scent of basil. I'm shaking all over, I can't talk. He lowers his head still more. Head down, just the top of his head shows. I see the white and red beads under his knit shirt. Xangô's sign. He looks at me, looking, what do you want, lady? I only wanted to know when you, that is, you, sir, when's the next time you're going to dance. He calls the waiter, pays the bill, leaves. His glass full, on top of the table. Warrior of Xangô, where are your wars? He leaves, moves of a dancer, the scent of basil in the air. Under the slow fluttering of the wide brim of his straw hat, smiling the smile of still water. You said you'd pray for me in the sanctuary, when you went back home. The good-looking black man moves away, toward Cathedral Square, moves of a dancer, head high, standing out among the people in the street. He's going. Warrior of Xangô, where are your wars? Where is your kingdom? King of the lightning and of the thunderbolts. Xangô, your father. Who knows my destiny, my fate, my future? I don't want to know, because I know already.

32

I open the window. The wind from off the sea embraces my body, sprawling in surrender on the fur rug. The scent of ripe fruit. I feel a dizziness. Distant drums cut through the night, penetrate my skin, the inner recesses of my invaded pores. This beating of far-off drums speaks to innumerable nights in immemorial time. Where does the beating come from, carried on the wind from off the sea? The night is magical, the night is immense. Whose hands are on the drums? Whose feet are these dancing? Whose bodies are these, fallen into a trance? My body trembles, I pull my body in between my hands and feet. The night is magical, the night is immense. My panting sex. The slender leaves of the sacred mango tree, quivering, with a dry sound in among the protected nests. The telephone. I don't answer. The ringing. I don't get up. I won't answer for anyone. Where's the good-looking black man, moves of a dancer, scent of basil? Under his knit shirt, the white beads, the red beads. Xangô's colors. The rippling muscles under his lustrous skin, so smooth. Xangô, the god of lightning and thunder. The good-looking black man, the son of Xangô, the white beads, the red beads. The wind from off the sea invades the inner recesses of my pores. The scent of ripe fruit wafts in on the wind from off the sea. I feel a dizziness. The drums are beating in the black night. Where is it coming from, this beating that the wind from off the sea brings? The night is magical, the night is immense. Where is the good-looking black man, moves of a dancer, scent of basil? King of the thunder and lightning, where is his realm? Where is the sky of his lightning, where does his thunder roar? A gentle rain falling softly on the sacred mango tree. The ripe fruit, moist in the cold night. Where is the beat of the beaten drums I can't hear? I go to the window. I let the rain fall full against my body. A gentle rain falling gently on my body in flames. The rainwater embraces my body. The evening chill. I'm cold. I turn around and open up my mirrors. The drops of water glisten even more in the sheen of the cold glass. I put on my robe and shield myself against the unwarmed images. My eyes seek one another out in the retreating images. I'm seeking what I'm not seeking. I'm not seeking what I'm seeking. I know what I'll find in the irrevocable flight of the mirrors. I know what I won't find. I comb out my hair, tie my robe, my face, cold, is explained. The good-looking black man flashes by in a series of images. Good-looking. Black. I tie my robe tighter. I don't tremble. I'm strong and tough, in command of my own body and my fate. The good-looking black man is a good-looking black man. The series of images vanishes and I see my cold face. The drums silent in the black night. No scent in the air. I gaze at my gaze in the unfolding of the mirrors. I'm here. I'm there. A woman, in firm command of my battles, my body, my fate. I. I'm not out to find any man who's not out to find me. Once more, the faint beat of the far-off drums, ever deeper in the many nights. The penetrating scent of ripe mangoes. I recognize the wind from off the sea and my fixed gaze, in the flight of the mirrors. I see a tired face emerging from the robe. The woman who writes me is there. But she doesn't laugh at my humiliation. I won't think any more about the good-looking black man, moves of a dancer, scent of basil.

The woman who writes me doesn't laugh at my humiliation. She still doesn't want to confess her disappointment. Fatigue and boredom. She's trying to survive in the arms of her schoolteacher husband. His thin arms smothered in his striped pajamas. He likes everything to be in apple-pie order. He likes Home Sweet Home and no going out on Saturday nights. Once a week they go to the movies. Once a week they visit an elderly aunt. Once a week they make love. Once a week they eat fish. The tired face pressed to the mirror, whose is it? Rats run around the yard of the little house in Brotas. The woman who writes me looks at her feet and puts on her stockings. Her schoolteacher husband says it's a good idea to sleep with your stockings on. It keeps your feet from getting cold. She thinks of rats.

I close the mirrors.

I close the windows.

My legs are closed, my feet are intact, firm.

I can't make fun of the woman who writes me. I can't do to her what she did to me. If she can't maintain the illusion of her marriage, she'll die. She won't be able to put me on paper any more. We live off our own deaths. Her saying yes. Me saying no. We have to live out our illusions to the end. Until the circle closes. Or until it opens, to start in again. We start in on only what we've finished. The rats that finished on my feet have started in on hers. One by one. Rat and foot. As long as she sleeps with her stockings on to please her schoolteacher husband, the rats won't bother her. They'll run around in the yard and she'll say it's the wind in the mango tree. As long as I defend my right to open and close my mirrors, whenever I want to, without thinking about my wayward sons, there'll be no rats under my bed. She, the woman who writes me, since she has no children of her own, thinks about mine.

You can't go on turning a blind eye to your sons' tragedy. It's not right for you to say they're beyond saving. Your oldest son didn't have to be hospitalized for drugs, because he wasn't even addicted. It's true for some time he experimented, but he came to his senses, changed his ways and even broke off with his bad friends. Now he wants to go back to school, wants to take the college entrance exams, he's confused, can't count on his father, he's ashamed of his mother, who has been running around hopping in bed with every man she meets, causing people to talk and, as if that weren't enough, has just fallen for a low-class black man who can't even speak the language properly. Your middle son is not a homosexual, as some people thought, because he's the "sensitive" type and also because of some dubious friendships. Everybody knew it was absolutely unfair to arrest him. They proved the whole thing was nothing more than a minor scuffle and the court let him off. Your indifference and your irresponsibility can, despite everything, push your son into homosexuality, while some simple concern might be enough to encourage his vocation for the theatre. You know very well that your husband lacked any background for understanding a son who wanted to study ballet and had friends in the arts who sometimes wore rather outré clothes and said things that a father and mother weren't used to hearing and were shocked at. Your three sons are rebellious because their friends say their mother has turned into a whore. You saw what your youngest one did. He nearly killed that bastard of a novelist who was with you that night. You did everything possible to convince yourself the boy was drunk, but you know it's not true. He couldn't stand being ridiculed by his friends and

117

he went home all set to do away with you and whoever was with you. With the excuse you had to go make him some coffee, you pretend that they didn't come to blows. You know that if your boyfriend weren't a skilled capoeira *fighter, you'd have a son wanted for murder. Just because the kid likes to take a drink, you call him an alcoholic. He's not addicted. Sometimes he has gone a bit too far, but he isn't anywhere near being an alcoholic. That is, he wouldn't be, if you didn't give him cause to rebel. It's absurd that your sons live with other people, when they have a home and a mother. All three have already gone through the phase of aggression and rebellion typical of adolescence and are looking for a way out. It will be your fault, your unpardonable crime, if the boys are ruined because of a mother who has lost her reputation and gets talked about all over town, for leading a scandalous, dissolute, not to say ridiculous life.*

I hate the woman who writes me. Once again, she has spoken, because I wanted her to. My desires lead her on the chain of my imagination. I wanted to hear her in her delirium, to have a notion of how much I really hate her. She hates me. We live. Each enslaved to the other.

My authoress just can't wait to finish this book. She looks at the pages written and sighs, not realizing what I know. I know what's necessary to move ahead with my story. Now the woman who writes me has other reasons to refuse to put me on paper. She thinks she should think she should always be at the beck and call of her schoolteacher husband's puny little machismo. He can't know she's writing. He wouldn't permit it. But she'll keep on writing me, no matter what he or she wants. She talks about my sons because that's what she wants. Also because I want her to want to, because I don't want to talk about them. Or think. They made their bed. I made mine. Consciously or unconsciously, each of us sets out an individual course. Choose your path. Choose it or is it chosen for you? Lines traced on the palm of your hand. The pattern revealed in the casting of seashells. The fortune of the cast when you cast your fortune. The mystery hidden in secret writing. The lord of time knows the answers the seashells provide. What about Xangô's son? Does he cast his fortune in the seashells' cast? Does he read secrets in the secrets of the shells? My fortune, my path in the pattern traced by lightning and thunder. A choice without a choice. I don't need secrets from seashells. I know my secret. My destiny. My waters. My fire. My mirrors.

33

My father planted sunflowers under the window of my room, in the townhouse in Rio Vermelho. Who planted the sacred mango tree the wind is now slicing into down below the window of my apartment on Seventh of September Avenue? Who's that down there all in white, looking like a king, moving like a dancer? Is he the one? A chill runs up and down my spine. I look again. He's standing motionless, under the sacred mango tree, every inch a king, the look of a warrior. The good-looking black man. Lord of the thunder and lightning. Standing underneath the sacred mango tree. Did he find out where I live? Is it possible? Do I go down? Or not? He's standing there, his head held high, at the peak of his arrogance. Warrior and king. Goose bumps. A feeling of warmth runs clear through my body. Do I go? Or not? I take the elevator down. Do I go out? I reach the door. He has his back to me, a few yards away. He turns around. He looks at me. Goose bumps. Walking up to him just then is a young black woman, all in white, moves of a dancer, flower in her hair, scent of lavender. He gives me a look, a close look. He puts his hand around the black girl's waist, the girl in white. The two of them walking toward me. Their look is lightning striking me. The two of them go by, both in white, moving like dancers, floating away in a pattern of receding waves, I'm rooted to the spot, the lightning sets me on fire in a storm of despair. A fine rain starts to send a slow chill through my veins.

On top of the small table on the fur rug are some copies of my book, which has just come out. The wind from off the sea rustles the bookcovers softly. A part of me is in there, part of my blood, part of my nerves, part of me saying yes, part saying no. My friends want to celebrate. And I'm a bunch of dead cells, somewhere between yes and no and perhaps. Consent, refusal, inertia. I want to be alone, solitary in my solitude, just me, just myself for company. My friends want to go out and celebrate. My first book. The wind from off the sea makes the bookcovers rustle softly. Yes, let's go out and celebrate. Where am I, if not here, in this seaside bar? The wind from off the sea isn't the wind from off the sea. A land of hot winds and tall drums and mysterious gods, on the other side of the Atlantic. On this side, hot winds and tall drums and mysterious gods, from over there, with the ocean in the middle. Where am I, if not here with my friends sitting around these three tables, in this seaside bar? Let's celebrate, she's earned it, long live the new authoress, another round of ice cold beer, congratulations, your book is a milestone, why didn't you publish this book before? I'm lonely in a crowd. I'm not here. Who am I with? What are we going to eat? When are you going to publish your next book? Who wants some crab in the shell? Get away from me, you'll be getting me all hot too. Where am I? The wind from off the sea isn't the wind from off the sea. If anyone wants to get really hot, just order the sea chowder, does everybody want some? So then what'll happen? Who's that, all in white, just came in by himself, over by the door? Is he the one? I don't look, because I don't want to. Storms are beginning to roar in the depths of my surprise. Goose bumps. Is he the one? I change places and keep my back to the tall black man in white. I don't look because I don't want to. Where am I, if not here? No, I'm not here. I'm not sandwiched in between my mirrors, with a mingle of faces multiplied over and over. Not here not there, space you can be in and not be in? Then where? Now is not now. Is he the one? No, I don't look, because I don't want to look. Why cast seashells to learn my fate? I don't need to cast shells to know my fate. My fate, the road I take. The storms are rumbling inside me. Aphrodisiac? Is sea chowder an aphrodisiac? None for me. She doesn't want any, she doesn't want any. I'm lonely in a crowd. If she has the sea chowder, who'll be able to handle this woman? I don't feel like laughing. I don't feel like talking. I don't feel like looking back, to keep from looking. Someone's there, coming closer. I shudder. Goose bumps. A tall black man in white. He speaks hurriedly with somebody in our group. I sigh. He's not the one. No, he's not the one. Who is the good-looking black man, son of the god Xangô, moves of a dancer, scent of basil? Who is he? Where am I, if I'm not here? I'm not here, sitting in this seaside bar, with my friends, celebrating the publication of my book. The wind from off the sea isn't the wind from off the sea. Why didn't I know the happiness I didn't know, when I saw this part of me in print? A bundle of dead cells, somewhere between no and yes and maybe. On the other side of the ocean, a raw-nerved land with hot winds and tall drums and mysterious gods. Where am I, if not here. No, it's not him, the good-looking black man, son of Xangô, god of lightning and thunder. Where is he, if he's not here? Who is he with, if he's with me? He's not here. And where am I? Storm-struck, I've no pride or shame, unless it's pride in my tanned skin, my curly hair. And the shame of not knowing the color of my great-great-grandfather's skin. The wind out of Africa blows through the coconut palms and my curly hair and the pages of my book. I tear out one by one the pages of my book, they take to the air, borne by the wind from afar, the wind that comes from the hot winds of the coast of Africa. I step away, alone, solitary in my solitude. Barefoot, the warm sand of the beach underfoot. Walking hard. Facing into the roar of the storms. Walking. Through the foam. Through the waves. Through the very depths of the ocean.

35

I know where the good-looking black man, the son of Xangô, lives. I know where he works. A maker of clay figures, molding shapes, solid hands making forms out of the formless mass. A dancer, making up new moves in response to the drums, winged feet in the African night. The magic night of his ancestors' music, called up by his father Xangô. I know where the priestess of his cult lives. Where the dance of Xangô is danced. Realm of the king of lightning and thunder.

I know where I am. The deep down rhythm of the drums, hands and feet thrusting out of the heart of the night. Out of her cloud of strings of charms and lace and embroidery, the priestess reverences her throne, starts up the singing and calls the gods down. The *orixás* make their swift way down. Night trembles in each one that descends to the temple floor. There's Xangô mounting his devotee like a horse, and hurling his bolts at the heavens. The good-looking black man. The good-looking black man? The god of lightning and thunder? Who dances, dancing to the beat of the deep drums pounded into the dark night? Night quivering, in the darkness of its heart. Time beyond all measure surrounds me and hurls me down into the formless depths. I know where I am. The deep rhythm of the drums, by lights that pierce the ancient night. I pull in on myself and everything in me comes together. The drums echoing through my taut body and hammering away at the pit of my stomach. The dense night. Xangô mounting his horse and dancing his dance and hurling his lightning bolts. The good-looking black man is the good-looking black man, the horse of Xangô. The drums diving deeper into the pit of my stomach. The red beads, the white beads clicking in the night, in the dance, in the trance, in the clouds of lace, in the feet on the hard clay floor. The drums are beating faster. Lightning bolts from Xangô's hands dart into the midst of red beads, of white beads. The heavy beat of the drums echoes in my chest working hard for breath. Bathed in sweat and sound, I know where I am, in this timeless, formless night, I know, I close my eyes, hands and feet thrusting out of the heart of the night, night striking me full on the chest, I'm reeling, I keel over backward, I quiver and shake, I'm gone, where am I? The trance.

Does she belong to Oxum? To Yansan? She belongs to Oxum. Yansan is her mistress. She's got to start her preparations for initiation. She'll die, if she doesn't want to be Oxum's horse. If she doesn't want to be Yansan's horse. Power over the waters. Power over the winds and storms. Oxum. Yansan. Hers are the graceful moves. Hers is the war cry. Oxum. Yansan. She understands gentle things. She disperses the storms. The golden yellows. The bloody reds. She belongs to Oxum. Yansan is her mistress. She'll die, if she doesn't begin her initiation.

I know where I am. The deep rhythm of the drums, hands and feet thrusting out of the heart of the night. Night starts in the pit of my stomach and ends on the other side of the ocean. It starts out on the other side of the ocean and ends in the pit of my stomach. Night lifted on high by the beating of the drums. The goddess of the waters. The goddess of the storms. My light and my death. My watery beads. My fiery beads. My decision and my fate. My peace and my war. I'm tied to the drums by a thread. My no and my yes. My exhaustion and my desire. My day and my night. Rain. Fire. The lightning of Xangô.

I know where I am. The clouds of embroidery and lace gently swaying. I snuggle into her starched petticoats. I hold onto the black hand, its warm roughness. I snuggle deeper into the friendly crinkling of starched embroidery. The peaceful swing of the charm beads. If you don't want to die, you have to begin your initiation. Or you'll pay for it later. Your fate, the road you'll take. You begin your initiation. Or you'll die. My fate, the road I'll take.

The good-looking black man, the son of Xangô, gives me a look, a good close look. I smile without smiling. I've got to get out of here. I can't drive. The good-looking black man looking at me, looking me over. He's telling me he'll take me. He can drive my car. He knows where I live. He smiles without smiling. His white outfit. The red beads, the white beads. I'm exhausted. The trance. In the pit of my stomach there's still an echo of beating drums. My body aches from the savage rhythm. The wind that comes from the wind refreshes my sweaty body. The good-looking black man, moves of a dancer, smelling of Xangô, takes me off into the night. He drives my car. Into the heart of the immense night. The black night. The magic night. The motion of my car. The beat of my heart. The rhythm of Xangô. I let myself be taken off into the night. Into the hot night, the smell of basil and sweat. I come back from my exhaustion in the wind that comes from the wind, in the night filled with night. The good-looking black man dressed in white. The strands of red beads. The strands of white beads. The good-looking black man is a good-looking black man. I shiver in the heart of night. He goes up to my apartment with me. Moves of a dancer, the walk of a king, a warrior at rest. I open the window. The wind from off the sea, comes from the sea, comes from the wind from the distant land, on the far side of the ocean. From the sacred mango tree comes the scent of ripe fruit. The ancient night. Total silence, no wind, no thought. Silence punctuated only by the sound of blood running faster in my eager veins. Night beyond time and shape thunders and lightnings in my core. Streaks of lightning softly penetrate into every corner of my being, primal drives and burning torrents flooding me. Breaking the black silence, the gasping of the storm and finally the quick flash of a scream piercing to the very roots of night. On the fur rug, the good-looking body of the good-looking black man. The horizontal rhythm of his muscles. Vertically the rhythmic breathing. The smell of basil and sweat, coupled with the full-bodied scent of ripe mango. The wind from off the sea comes from the sea and from the storm and the hidden lightning. On the sofa, the white clothes thrown down over the red beads and white beads. My night is at rest, in the heart of the black night. But night, the heavy silence, the smells and once more the blood running faster in the eager veins, the primal force, the primal power, the purity of the elements, the streaks of lightning, the flood of burning torrents, the gasping of the storm, and finally, once again, night transfixed by the scream beyond all.

Mango, sweat, basil.

So what now? I know where I am in this my present situation. Fulfilled and total. I'm here. Whole and multiple. Complete. My whole body centered upon its rich and solid expectation. Curled up on the fur rug, my solitude has company. Things to think about. The new-found fragrance of my pores. He's not here, but he is here. Whole, complete. My whole being responds to the echo of his presence with me, the primal drive added to my desire. He transported me. He fulfilled me. What words could possibly express it? It's what happened. Lightning and thunder, in a line of storms. In the concave and the convex of my waters. In the spread of my firestorms. The king takes possession. Peace in war.

I wait. Whole and multiple. Complete.

He went away, deep in silence. Looking at me to keep from looking. Smiling to keep from smiling. Protected by his charm beads. Red and white. Dressed in white, moves of a dancer, a warrior, the bearing of a king. He went away, his scent a trail behind him. Sweat and basil. He looked at me. Looking to keep from looking. He smiled. Smiling to keep from smiling. He picked up his beads. His body glistened, in the sudden quick flash of lightning. In the instant roll of thunder. He went away.

I wait in the primitive night of my desire. A maelstrom. Wildfire breaking loose. The distant drums slicing through the dark space interrupted by street lamps and stars. Whose hands are on the drums? Whose feet are dancing? The tall drums of Xangô. Where is the son of Xangô, who's not here? But he is here. He went away deep in silence, with his dancer's moves. To the sound of his clean smell. Sweat and basil.

I wait. Whole and multiple. Complete.

I wait. Choking from the cloying scent of sweat and basil. Night is when I touch bottom. Life and death. Good and evil. The scent of ripe fruit comes from the sacred mango tree. The wind from off the sea, what sea is it? The wave down on the beach struck beaches on the far side of the ocean. The beating of the distant drums weaves a net in the dark night. He went away, deep in his heavy silence. Silence filled with words, always just beneath the surface. I wait. Curled up on the fur rug. Heat. Cold. Emptiness. Fullness. Protected by her starched petticoats. Coziness. Cloud of charm beads and lace and embroidery. Why don't I go? Casting seashells. I don't need to know the secret of the seashells. I know my secret. My fate. My choice. My colors. My waters. My fire. My mirrors.

The wind from off the sea doesn't bring the scent of basil. The scent of basil seeps through my house, my living room, my bedroom, down into my private places, my sanctum, my impassable barriers. It comes in, past the point of no return. Possesses me. No other way. My choice. My waters. My fire. My mirrors. I'm the image and the projection of the images. Running away is death. Being here, being many. Being absent, being one. Waiting.

I wait.

The woman who writes me waits. She's waiting for her husband the schoolteacher to be through grading the exams. Today's the day. Her scent is soap and talcum powder. His scent is deodorant and toothpaste. She waits. He's just about through grading the exams. She goes to her bedroom, takes off her robe, doesn't unbutton her loose, long-sleeved nightgown. She sits down. She waits. She lies down. She waits. She gets up. She waits. She goes back to the living room. She keeps quiet. He doesn't like to be interrupted. He likes decent, docile women. He pretends he doesn't know about her past. She pretends she doesn't know he's pretending he doesn't know. She and he pretend they don't know today is the day. Everything should take place naturally, nothing to get nervous over. She so decent and proper. He so respectful and discreet. She goes back to the bedroom. He's almost through grading the exams. She sits down. She waits. She lies down. She waits. She gets up. She goes back to the living room. He's finished the last exam. He yawns. He gets up. Buttons up the top button of his striped pajamas. He asks for some herb tea. He's tired, needs to get some sleep. Did he forget or did he pretend he forgot? She doesn't pretend she believes him. She moves up close to the striped pajama pants encasing his thin legs. Lights go off. The two of them under the sheets. Their nightclothes kept on. Everything very proper. Very discreet. The rats, multiplying, lurking in the yard, scratching at the bedroom door. The scent of cologne. He works away. She waits under the sheets. The rats gnawing at the door. She didn't take her hose off. He keeps working away. He couldn't pretend he forgot today's the day. She's waiting. Respectful caresses. Her delicate suggestion he take off his glasses. His body on top of hers. A brief heaviness. Almost as if a man weren't inside a woman. A quick sigh from him. Not so much as ah out of her. The sweetish smell of cologne. The rats coming into the bedroom. She curls up, using her hands, afraid the rats might gnaw at her sex.

The night drives down into itself. The wind thrusts into the hollows of the leaves. Curled up alone on the fur rug, I wait. What am I waiting for? The ritual drums piercing the vast night. Far off. Whose hands are on the drums? Whose feet are dancing? The wind from off the sea comes from the sea of a distant land, tall drums, hot winds, mysterious gods. Xangô readies his lightning bolts. Oxum fleeing in the waters. Yansan knows about war. Cloud of charms and lace and embroidery. Why don't I go? The priestess starts up the singing, calling down the gods. The trance. Why don't I go? The warm security of those starched petticoats. If I don't go, I'll die. I've got to begin my initiation. Oxum. Yansan. My secret. My fate. If I don't get started with my initiation, I'll die. The road I take. Xangô readies his lightning bolts. The smell of ripe fruit. Solitary solitude. The cloying smell of sweat and basil. My blood runs faster. My lonely skin. My solitary pores. I wait. What am I waiting for? Xangô readies his lightning bolts.

I wait.

38

I don't wait. I stay put. In the loneliness of the smell of ripe mango wafted in on the wind. Wind that comes from the hot wind from the burning land of tall drums and powerful gods. Invincible. Warrior gods. Kingly gods. Lordly gods of the natural and supernatural powers. Master gods of human destiny. Who decreed my fate? The fate that only unfolds hour by hour. Even in hours spent waiting. In vain, as if there were no hope. In vain. My fate. My choice. The good-looking black man, son of Xangô. My choice. My fate. My fate to belong to his fate. The young black girl, all in white, flower in her hair, scent of lavender. There they go, in the shade of the ancient mango tree, moves of dancers, choice, fate. Lines and links and knots and ties bound up in the casting of seashells. A design designed in advance. The seashells don't mean I'm not free. I am free. To pursue my fate. In the lonely smell of ripe fruit? In the comforting warmth of starched petticoats? The rhythm of the beads. The powerful gods can't change my fate. I'm not the young black girl, all in white, flower in her hair, scent of lavender. The powerful gods can't change my destiny. The road I take. My choice.

I don't open the door. I don't answer the telephone. I don't want to see anyone. I don't look for my images inside the mirrors. Lying on the sofa, my eyes closed, motionless, I know it's night.

I don't wait.

No, I don't wait. Exhaustion. Weariness. Boredom. So far away, the magic night. So far away, the sacred dance. The trance. The drums beating in the depths of the night. The drums beating in the pit of my stomach. Xangô's lightning. My pulse racing to the rhythm of the drums. Lights going out. The hard clay floor vanishing under my feet. My head spinning in the circle around the deities. The trance. Where am I? The rhythm of the charm beads. The beat of the temple drums in the night, in my core. The cloud of beads and lace and embroidery. If she doesn't begin her initiation, she'll die. Oxum. Yansan. My head. Water and fire. My life hangs by a thread. The thread from the drums. Xangô readies his lightning bolts. The drum beat echoing in my core. Only my exhaustion keeps me clinging to the night and to life. Exhaustion. The look from Xangô's son. The look looking to look me over. The smile not smiling in order to smile. The reach of Xangô's lightning. Never again will I see this look looking at me to look me over, entering me, possessing me. Lightning and thunder. Water and fire. Storm. Not ever again. He went away, heavy silence, moves of a dancer, the red beads, the white beads. Amid the sudden streaks of lightning. In the instant roll of thunder. I'm filled to the full, resting on the fur rug. A fresh encounter, plunging to the utmost depths of my waters, my night, my storm, my roots. The glow from a fire that burned down to nothing. I know the very heart of knowing. And because I know, I don't know. And because I don't know, I must forget. And since I can't forget, I can't forget. The exhaustion. The exhaustion eating into me. The weariness. The utter tedium.

Someone's ringing the doorbell. I don't move. The doorbell keeps on ringing. I don't want to know who it is. I don't want to see anyone. Someone pounding loudly with their hands. I don't move. Stopped cold, stark frozen in the rootless night. Who's that who won't quit pounding and pounding away? It sounds like someone trying to knock the door down. The nervous edge in the voice of my youngest son. Shouting from outside. It's been so long since I heard anyone say mother. It's been so long since I said mother. I wonder what my son wants. He sounds different. Please, let me in. I don't move. For God's sake, let me in. You're at home. I don't move, frozen in my night with nothing left for me. He's pounding, screaming. Maybe he's got a gun. Maybe he's drunk. Maybe he's out to kill me. I'm dying of exhaustion. I can't move a muscle. He keeps on pounding, calling me, screaming, crying. I'm worn out. Silence oozes out. My nerves are frayed, I'm turning to jelly. Utter tedium. Thick heavy silence. No fire no water. No storm no showers. No wind from off the sea. No smell of ripe fruit. No scent of basil.

The rats made their way into the house of the woman who writes me. She took off her hose to go to bed. She stopped visiting her husband's elderly aunt. The white window curtains are torn. The crocheted doilies trimming the trays and kitchen shelves are dirty. She left and didn't come back for dinner. She doesn't want to sleep with her husband the schoolteacher any more. His solemn bones poke holes in her wasted body. She doesn't know what to expect. She doesn't know what not to expect. Now, in the living room, the rats started to gnaw at her feet. She's sorry it disgusts her to see that thin, withered man walking around the house in his striped pajamas, bleary eyes hidden behind his glasses, smelling of cheap deodorant.

Why did my son come and pound on my door, so late at night? The clammy, sticky night. Could it be he was running away from some kind of danger? I'm still leaden on the sofa. The same exhaustion. Just plain worn out. The ancient mango tree doesn't rustle its leaves. Stock still in the night, crystallized in time. The sudden noise of voices in the street. Two men talking, shouting, fighting. Do I know these voices? Voices stabbing into the edgy night. Shots streaking through the night. All those voices in the slippery night. Early morning traffic moving in the street. I don't move. A sticky wind wafts me the smell of something rotten.

40

I turn on the radio, to the news. Perhaps they'll have something about last night's fight. Were those shots? I don't hear what I'm hearing. A deranged young man, from one of the old-line families of our city, defending his mother's reputation, has lost his life. The police have no clues. An appeal to the young man's parents to come identify the body.

I can't walk, my feet gnawed at by rats. They come at night. Real rats. Gnawing at my feet. Gnawing at my sex. The woman who writes me is sitting down, also unable to walk, her feet gnawed at by rats. Real rats. She didn't want to open the door for my son. She was afraid her husband the school-teacher would get the wrong idea about her reputation as a married woman. Though he pretended he didn't, he knew that in the last few years she'd been interested in young men. She couldn't take a chance, especially now they were separating. She wanted to leave her husband without giving him grounds to suspect that she'd been unfaithful to him. She refused to open the door for my son. He only wanted help, a word of support.

Your son was desperate. His friends teased him, saying you went out with every man who came along, even black men from the candomblé. *That night, your son was carrying a gun. He was about to go into his mother's apartment building, when he saw at the door a tall black man, all in white. There was a struggle. The black man took his revolver. Someone called the police. He went on into the building. You refused to let your own son in. He went away with nowhere to turn. As he left, to keep from being arrested, he put up a fight. They shot him.*

The woman who writes me knows that, if she had let my son in, none of this need ever have happened. The woman who writes me is devoured with guilt. She refuses to write me. It's all right. My story is just about over. Everything I could have wanted to try, I tried. It's all over. We've followed our footsteps right down to the last one. Now we're standing here, each looking at the other, our feet gnawed at by rats. The mirrors multiply our images ad infinitum. But our guilt brings us together. The rat smell drives out the scent that comes from the ancient mango tree. My face in the mirror is her face. I'm her. She's me. We are one. Shoulders sagging. Eyes to the floor. The intersection of me-with-her turned into me-with-me. We are one. Me and *me*. Me. ME. Dead center. The mirrors give off an intolerable glare. Frozen. I see more than I see. Eye to eye. Bedrock. I write what I write. I.

Outside the lightning starts to flash. The sudden thunderclaps respond with a deafening roll. The mirrors send back and forth the same pulled-down, pent-up face, without so much as a quiver. The storm. The open mirrors. The open window. Suddenly a lightning bolt streaks across the dark sky. The mirrors shatter into a thousand pieces. On the floor, shards of mirror wet with blood. Wet with rainwater. A flicker of fire shoots skyward. I see an entire face in a shard of glass. A single face. I can't identify the smell coming in on the wind. The face. Me. The gentle wind from out of the heavy storm.